The Last Hands

Garvey T. Avon

CA&C Audio Productions

This is a work of fiction. Names, characters, businesses, places, events, locales, and incidents are either the products of the author's imagination or used in a fictitious manner. Any resemblance to actual persons, living or dead, or actual events is purely coincidental.

CONTENT WARNING: The main character in this book has survived significant abuse. She flashes back to these memories and relieves some of the experiences in her dreams. If this may be triggering for you, please put your mental health first and proceed with caution or skip this story completely.[3]

eBook Edition ISBN-13 978-1-971094-00-7

Audiobook ISBN-13 978-1-971094-01-4

Cover design by Jermaine Haggerty

Contents

Chapter 1 – The Invitation

- -

She called the final bet, her voice steady and controlled in the velvet silence of the Bellagio poker room. The air hung thick with cigar smoke and desperation, the clink of ice in a distant glass echoing like a gunshot in the stillness. Across the green felt, Novo Petrovich, a man whose face was carved from Siberian granite, didn't flinch. He pushed his remaining chips forward, a mountain of crimson and ivory plastic, sealing his fate. Destiny's dark eyes didn't leave his, but her focus narrowed to the microscopic tremor in the muscle beneath his left eye. A tell. Not fear, not exactly. Resignation. He knew. He'd been outplayed.

"All in," Novo rasped, defeat heavy in his voice.

Destiny turned her cards. Ace of spades. King of hearts. Novo's shoulders slumped a fraction further as he revealed his pair of tens. The river card was a meaningless three of diamonds. A collective breath hissed out from the railbirds watching. Five hundred thousand dollars. The dealer pushed the towering pile of chips towards her, a landslide of potential. A ripple of applause, polite, edged with envy, washed over the table. Destiny offered Novo a curt nod, the minimal courtesy required. No gloating. Gloating was for amateurs and fools. She gathered her chips, her movements economical, precise. The weight of them, the sheer physicality of half a million dollars, was a familiar anchor.

What her opponents never understood was the pattern behind her play. The mathematical symmetry her father had drilled into her since she was nine. "Poker isn't just cards, brilliant girl," he'd say, demonstrating complex betting patterns that seemed random but followed a precise mathematical sequence. "It's a language all its own. Remember the patterns. They're the key to everything." Those lessons were embedded in her neural pathways now, an unconscious architecture underlying every hand she played. Her signature style that had become her calling card on the circuit.

Two hours later, The adrenaline crash left her restless and empty. The penthouse suite at the Bellagio, comped for high rollers, felt less like a reward and more like another impersonal box. Floor-to-ceiling windows showcased the garish neon symphony of the Strip, a perpetual twilight that never slept. Destiny bypassed the minibar, the plush sofas, the king-sized bed. She stood at the window, the city's frantic energy buzzing against the thick glass, a world away. Her reflection stared back – a woman in a sharp black jumpsuit, her hair pulled back in a severe knot that emphasized high cheekbones and dark eyes that held too much calculation, too much guarded history. She touched the emerald stud in her left earlobe, the stone cool and smooth against her fingertip. The other earring was identical, a matched pair. Her father's voice, warm and gravelly, ghosted through her mind. *For my brilliant girl. Emeralds for wisdom, for seeing what others miss.* She was twelve. He was dead a week later. Car accident—though she'd never believed it was that simple.

She turned away from the glittering facade of Vegas. Her actual residence was a high-rise condo fifteen minutes off the Strip, all clean lines, white surfaces, and a view almost as expansive. It wasn't a home. It was a waystation. A place to sleep, to shower, to strategize the next game. The walls held no photographs, no souvenirs. Just a boxing bag hanging in the spare room and shelves lined with books on game theory, psychology, and the cold elegance of mathematics. She'd walked away from her PhD at MIT because the pure abstraction of numbers felt suddenly meaningless after the brutal finality of her father's death. Probability couldn't predict a drunk driver. Poker, though... poker was math made visceral. It was probability you could *feel* in the sweat on an opponent's brow, the hitch in their breath, the desperate flicker in their eyes. It was control.

She remembered how the financial aid office had become as familiar as her dorm room. Destiny would sit across from Mrs. Patel, watching her tap numbers into a calculator with crimson fingernails. "Even with your scholarships and these loans, there's still a gap," Mrs. Patel would say, her voice softening with genuine concern. Destiny learned to nod stoically, to save her tears for the walk back across campus.

By her junior year, Destiny's daily routine had become a precarious balancing act. Mornings at the campus coffee shop, afternoons at the library desk, and weekend nights bartending at The Rusty Nail. Her textbooks remained open on breaks, highlighted passages blurring as exhaustion set in. Sleep became a luxury she could rarely afford, while her classmates discussed spring break plans and new apartments.

The twenty-first birthday lottery ticket was her mother's idea—tucked inside a card with a lipstick kiss and a twenty-dollar bill. "For something fun," the note read. Destiny had smiled weakly, knowing the twenty would go toward her overdue electric bill. The five-dollar scratch ticket seemed like an extravagance, but something about her mother's hopeful handwriting made her keep it.

Three days later, while waiting for the bus in freezing rain, she remembered the ticket. Under the shelter's flickering light, she scratched away the silver coating with a house key. The numbers aligned in a way that didn't register at first—her mind refusing to process what her eyes were seeing. She checked it four times, hands trembling, before showing it to the convenience store clerk.

The $2,800 check arrived a week later. For the first time in two years, Destiny paid her rent early. She bought groceries without calculating the total as she shopped. She replaced her worn-out winter boots. Most significantly, she slept through the night, the perpetual knot in her stomach temporarily unraveled.

But it was the mathematics that truly seduced her. Five dollars transformed into twenty-eight hundred. A 560-fold return that defied everything her economics professor preached about rational markets and reasonable expectations. The statistical improbability of her win presented an intoxicating alternative narrative—that perhaps the universe operated on different principles for different people.

The knock on her door was sharp and unexpected, bringing her back to the present. Not the building's discreet concierge. This was urgent. Destiny moved quietly, her boxer's instincts humming. She peered through the fisheye lens. A courier, anonymous in a dark uniform, holding a slim, matte-black envelope. No logo. Her pulse, steady since leaving the casino, gave a single, hard thump against her ribs. This felt deliberate.

She opened the door a crack, the security chain engaged. "Yes?"

The courier didn't meet her eyes. "Delivery for Destiny Rivers. Requires signature." He held out an electronic pad. His hands were steady, clean. Too clean for a bike courier in Vegas heat. Destiny scanned his posture. Not the weary slump of a courier, but the coiled stillness of a fighter waiting for the bell. His weight was balanced, his shoulders back. He wasn't delivering a package; he was holding a position.

She signed a meaningless squiggle. The courier handed her the envelope, turned, and was gone, disappearing into the elevator bank without a backward glance. Destiny closed the door, locked it, engaged the deadbolt. The envelope felt heavy, expensive cardstock. She slit it open with a fingernail.

Inside, a single sheet of thick, cream-colored paper. Elegant, embossed lettering at the top: *The Royal Meridian Invitational*. Below, impossible words:

No contact number. No website. Just a date, three days hence, and a terrifyingly blank space for her signature. A phone number, unlisted, presumably, was handwritten in precise, black ink at the bottom. Ten million dollars. It was ludicrous. High-stakes games existed, sure, but nothing like this. The buy-in alone was the GDP of a small island nation. It screamed trap. Something deeply, lethally wrong.

Logic demanded retreat. Every indicator signaled danger—the isolated location, the anonymous courier, the impossible stakes. But then... the prize. *Minimum* one hundred million. The zeroes stretched out in her mind, a vast, shimmering plain. One hundred million dollars wasn't just money. It was permanence. It was a fortress by the sea, walls thick enough to keep the world out. It was silence, and safety, and roots that went down deep. A *home*. She could picture it: sunlight on real wood floors, the smell of old books and coffee, a place where she could finally unpack the suitcase she'd been carrying since she was twelve. A place where the ghost of her father might find peace.

The emerald at her ear felt suddenly warm, a tiny point of heat against her skin. *For my brilliant girl.* Could she see what others missed? Could she see a way through the obvious danger to the impossible prize? Her fingers traced the embossed letters on the invitation. The risk assessment warred with the bone-deep yearning. The analytical part of her brain cataloged the terrifying variables. The wounded twelve-year-old girl whispered, *What if it's real? What if this is your way out?*

She walked to the window again, the invitation clenched in her hand. The neon glow of the Strip seemed garish, cheap, a desperate imitation of permanence. Below, people scurried like ants, chasing small dreams, small wins. She'd just won half a million dollars, and it felt like pocket change. Chump change. This... this was the big league. The ultimate gamble. Trusting this invitation felt like stepping off a cliff blindfolded. But staying here, playing the circuit, grinding out wins that only bought temporary distance... that felt like dying slowly. Like letting her father's ghost, and her own fear, win.

Her phone felt heavy in her pocket. She pulled it out, stared at the unlisted number written on the invitation. Her thumb hovered. Logic shrieked a final warning. Her heart hammered. The image of the sunlit room, the deep roots, the silence... it drowned out the noise. She dialed.

A single ring. Then a smooth, unaccented male voice. "Confirmation?"

Destiny took a breath, the air tasting of ozone and recklessness. "Yes."

"A car will collect you from your residence tomorrow at 0700. Pack for three days. Bring only personal effects. Funds will be verified upon boarding." The line went dead.

The silence in the minimalist apartment was absolute. She'd done it. She'd stepped off the cliff. The dread was a cold stone in her stomach, but beneath it, fierce and undeniable, fluttered a treacherous wing of hope.

The next thirty-six hours passed in a blur of unsettling efficiency. The car that collected her was a black SUV with tinted windows so dark they swallowed the desert dawn. The driver, another silent, broad-shouldered man with the same unnerving stillness as the courier, didn't speak. He drove, taking corners without the slightest swerve, to a private airfield north of the city. A sleek Gulfstream G650 waited on the tarmac, engines idling with a low, powerful thrum. No flight attendants, just the pilot and co-pilot, visible only as silhouettes behind the cockpit glass. The interior was cool leather and polished wood, luxurious but sterile. Destiny buckled in, the enormity of her decision pressing down on her. She touched her earring again, the emerald cool now. *See what others miss.* What was she missing? The isolation was complete. No other players visible. Just her, the hushed crew, and the vast, empty sky.

The flight to Miami was smooth, unnervingly quiet. She dozed fitfully, haunted by fragmented dreams – her father's laugh, the screech of tires, the cold weight of poker chips morphing into bars of gold. Landing was seamless. Another anonymous SUV waited, whisking her through the humid Miami sprawl to another private dock. Not the glittering marinas of South Beach. This was industrial, functional, smelling of diesel and salt and rust. A sleek helicopter sat on a concrete pad, its rotor blades drooping like the wings of a resting hawk.

The flight over the open ocean was a gut-churning roar. The sun glinted off the waves. No land in sight. Just water, stretching to the horizon in every direction. Then, it appeared. The *Royal Meridian*. It wasn't just a yacht. It was a floating city block, a leviathan of gleaming white steel and dark-tinted glass. Four decks rose like a stepped pyramid, crowned by a communications array that looked suspiciously robust for pleasure cruising. It wasn't just the size of the rig that snagged her attention, it was the jury-rigged quality of the fins bolted to the mast—ugly sheets of milled aluminum cut for brute-force output. Destiny recognized the design from SIG-INT white-papers: narrow-band L-block and Ku-block scramblers whose only job was to smother sat-phones and VSAT dishes inside a ten-mile bubble. All stick, no finesse.

Whoever built the array had trusted sheer wattage more than engineering

The helicopter descended towards the vast helipad. Destiny's stomach clenched. This was it. The point of no return. The helo settled with a soft thump. The door slid open. Warm, salt-tinged air rushed in. A man stood waiting on the immaculate deck, dressed in crisp white linen that should have looked relaxed but instead screamed uniform. He smiled, a perfectly calibrated expression of welcome.

"Ms. Rivers. Welcome aboard the *Royal Meridian*." His voice was smooth, practiced. "If you'll follow me, your cabin is ready. The verification of funds will commence shortly."

Destiny stepped out onto the deck. The yacht barely moved beneath her feet, a testament to its size and stabilizers. Sunlight bounced blindingly off the polished surfaces. It was opulent, breathtaking. A floating palace.

But as she followed the man in white, her senses, honed by years of reading the slightest flicker of deceit, went on high alert. She caught the subtle bulge beneath the jacket of a man polishing a railing – too angular for a radio. Another, adjusting a coiled rope, moved with the economical grace of someone trained to disarm and kill. The smiles offered were fleeting, professional masks. The polished deck felt less like a welcome mat and more like the lid of a very expensive, very dangerous box.

A door opened ahead of them, momentarily revealing what looked like a military command center hidden within the yacht's opulent interior. Three technicians in black polo shirts sat before banks of monitors, their screens displaying what appeared to be signal readouts, surveillance feeds, and satellite data. One technician was manipulating what looked like a 3D model of the surrounding ocean, with a red circle marking a large exclusion zone around their position. Another was monitoring what appeared to be communication frequencies, actively jamming signals.

The tech looked up, alarm flashing across his face as he spotted Destiny. "Sir, unauthorized—"

The door quickly closed, but not before a tall woman in a headset made eye contact with Destiny, her gaze cold and assessing.

Her guide accelerated slightly, as though pretending the glimpse had never happened. "Your suite is just ahead, Ms. Rivers."

"What was that room?" Destiny asked, her tone deliberately casual.

"Communications center," the man replied smoothly. "Mr. Harrison conducts business throughout his voyages. State-of-the-art equipment ensures uninterrupted connectivity despite our remote location."

The lie was polished, practiced. But Destiny had seen the satellite imagery, the weapons-grade communication jammers, the security protocols scrolling across the screens. This wasn't business connectivity. This was military-grade isolation enforcement.

Chapter 2 – Into Deep Waters

- -

Destiny followed the man in white through the gleaming corridors. Light streamed through vast windows, revealing endless ocean beyond. The silence pressed in, thick with hidden engines and watchful crew. Every polished surface reflected her tense expression."

Her cabin was a suite worthy of a five-star hotel, all muted tones and minimalist luxury. Her single bag sat on a luggage rack, looking absurdly small and vulnerable. The verification of funds had been clinical, efficient. A silent woman in a dark suit had scanned her retinal patterns and taken a blood sample – "Biometric security protocol," she'd stated flatly. Destiny hadn't argued. Arguing felt like poking a sleeping predator. The ten million was confirmed, transferred before she'd even boarded. The money was gone. She was locked in.

She unpacked: a few changes of clothes, toiletries, the worn copy of Sun Tzu's *The Art of War* that always traveled with her. Her fingers brushed the cool leather cover. *Know the enemy and know yourself.* Right now, she felt perilously known.. No phones. No internet terminals. Just the vast, isolating sea.

Dinner that evening was served in a dining salon overlooking a lower deck pool. Crystal chandeliers glittered overhead. Long tables draped in white linen were set with heavy silver and bone china. Perhaps thirty people were present – players, she assumed. The murmur of conversation was low and polite. Destiny scanned the room, her stare sharp, cataloging. Her poker face was in place, but beneath the calm mask, her mind raced, cataloging every tell.

Ryan Harrison commanded the head table. He wore a midnight blue suit that emphasized his formidable physique. His shaved head gleamed under the lights. He wasn't eating much, instead observing the room with the intensity of a chess master surveying his board. His smile, when he offered it to a passing server, was a calculated flash of white teeth that didn't reach his assessing eyes. Power radiated from him, not just wealth, but absolute authority. He caught Destiny's gaze across the room. A silent challenge. A predator acknowledging another predator. But there was something else there. Almost as if he were studying a long-awaited specimen. He tilted his head, watching her betting patterns during the small pre-dinner game at her table. His eyes narrowed at a particular sequence of bets she made—the Fibonacci progression her father had taught her. Something flickered across his face. She didn't look away, but a cold finger traced its way down her spine. He wasn't just a host. He was the warden.

Beside Harrison sat Celeste Montenegro. Wearing an elegant silver dress, her dark hair swept into an intricate chignon, she was breathtaking. She conversed animatedly with a man on her left, laughing with him that somehow felt rehearsed. But Destiny saw the calculation beneath the glamour. Celeste's hazel eyes missed nothing. They flickered constantly, assessing reactions, gauging tension, filing away information. She ran the surface of this operation with polished efficiency.

Harrison leaned toward Celeste, his public baritone softening into a more intimate, grounded cadence. "Watch that one," he murmured, his eyes still locked on Destiny. "Di gyal have a fire in her eye. A real fire."

Destiny noticed something else too—when Harrison's attention shifted elsewhere, Celeste's perfect smile faltered. For just a moment, her fingers tightened around her tablet before relaxing again. She resumed typing a heartbeat later, her composure perfect, but Destiny caught the flicker of something in her eyes. Not fear exactly. Something more complex.

Her scan continued. A man a few seats down from her own table caught her eye. Alex Morrison, according to the discreet name card. Mid-forties, expensive but ill-fitting suit, shoulders hunched. Sweat beaded his upper lip despite the air conditioning. He whispered something to the redhead beside him. She stiffened, shook her head. Alex flinched, knuckles white on his fork.

There was something familiar about his nervous mannerisms—the way he tapped his index finger twice before reaching for his water glass, the habit of adjusting his cufflinks when anxious. Fragments of childhood memory surfaced: a younger Alex, seated at her father's desk, going through financial reports. "Uncle Alex," her father had called him, though they weren't related. Her father's financial controller at the security firm. He'd brought her candy sometimes, asked about her math homework. After her father died, he'd disappeared from her life. A rabbit among wolves. Destiny filed him away.

Then he held her gaze at a table near the panoramic windows. Sitting alone, nursing a glass of bourbon was James "Shark" Williams. The sight of him was a punch to the gut. The legend looked diminished. The sharp, calculating eyes were still there, but they were shadowed. Deep lines etched his face, and his hands, resting on the tablecloth, trembled slightly. His clothes, once impeccably tailored, hung loosely on a frame that seemed to have shrunk. He looked like a man who hadn't slept in weeks. He looked broken. Their eyes met across the crowded room. Recognition flared in his, followed by a flicker of something desperate. He gave an almost imperceptible jerk of his head towards the doors leading to the outer deck. A silent summons.

Destiny excused herself with a murmured excuse about needing air. The transition from the brightly lit atmosphere of the dining room to the cool, salt-tinged darkness of the deck was jarring. The vastness of the ocean at night was terrifying. Black water stretched to a horizon indistinguishable from the starless sky. Only the yacht's running lights and the distant, indifferent pinpricks of stars broke the void. The hum of the engines was a constant vibration beneath her feet.

Shark materialized from the shadows near the railing, his face grim in the dim light spilling from the salon windows. He looked older up close.

"Destiny Rivers," he rasped. "Didn't think I'd see you here. Shouldn't be here. Shouldn't have come."

"Shark." Her voice was carefully neutral. "Long time. You look... well." The lie tasted flat.

He barked a harsh, humorless laugh. "Save it, kid. We both know I look like hell warmed over." He glanced over his shoulder towards the lit windows. "Listen to me. You need to get off this boat."

The cold dread in Destiny's stomach solidified. "The game hasn't even started."

"This isn't a game!" The whisper was fierce, edged with panic. "Not like any you've ever played. These people... Harrison..." He swallowed hard. "They're not hosting a tournament. They're testing. They're hunting."

"Hunting what?" Destiny kept her voice low and steady, though her pulse hammered against her ribs.

"Assets. Liabilities. Fucking entertainment?" Shark ran a trembling hand over his face. "I don't know exactly. But it's bad. Worse than bad. I'm in deep, Destiny. Owed money... bad people. Dangerous people. They own me. This... this was supposed to be my way out. But it's a trap. For all of us."

A chill deeper than the night air seeped into Destiny's bones. "Dangerous people? Who, Shark? Who owns you?" Her mind raced. Organized crime? Intelligence? Something else entirely?

He shook his head. "Can't say. Walls have ears. Literally, probably." He leaned closer, his breath smelling faintly of whiskey and fear. "Your father... Marcus. Brilliant man. Too smart for his own good sometimes. He knew things... saw things others missed. Like you."

He tapped his temple. "He warned me once, years ago. About getting in too deep with the wrong crowd. Should've listened." His eyes darted past her shoulder "Go. Now. Act normal."

Destiny didn't look back. She turned smoothly, her face a mask of bored indifference, and walked back towards the salon doors.

Inside, the clink of cutlery and low murmur of conversation seemed normal. She forced herself to breathe, to unclench her fists.

***

The poker tournament commenced the following evening in the grand salon. It had been transformed. The centerpiece was a vast, oval table crafted from a single slab of dark, polished wood, inlaid with subtle green felt playing surfaces at each position. Overhead, a constellation of recessed spotlights illuminated the table. High-backed leather chairs surrounded the table. The air hummed with suppressed tension, thick with the scent of expensive cigars and fine leather.

Celeste Montenegro glided to the center of the table, tablet in hand.

"Welcome to the Royal Meridian Invitational," she announced, her voice clear and measured.

"Sixteen players have qualified for this exclusive event. The tournament will progress over three days, with eliminations continuing until our final table of five players tomorrow evening. The championship will conclude on the final night, coinciding with our gala celebration."

She tapped her tablet, and the large screens around the salon illuminated with tournament brackets and chip counts.

"The blinds will begin at $100,000/$200,000 and increase every ninety minutes according to the schedule now displayed. As Mr. Harrison has explained, elimination is final. There are no rebuys or second chances." Her eyes swept the table with practiced neutrality. "The tournament prize pool stands at one hundred million dollars, with payouts beginning at the final table."

Destiny did the mental math—sixteen players, elimination structure, accelerating blinds. The tournament was designed to force aggressive play and rapid eliminations. By tomorrow night, most of them would be gone.

Destiny took her assigned seat. The other players were filtering in. A man with the name tag Ben looked even paler. His hands were visibly shaking as he fumbled with his chair. Celeste glided to a seat adjacent to Harrison's, a sleek tablet in hand.. Harrison himself took the head of the table, a king surveying his court.

Rubben Kane entered like he owned the room. He moved with a loose-limbed confidence, a stark contrast to the nervous energy of Ben or the brittle tension crackling through the room. He wore a charcoal suit that fit him like a second skin, emphasizing lean muscle. His dark hair was tousled, and his green eyes scanned the room with sharp, intelligent curiosity. As he approached, Destiny noted how his gaze paused briefly on each security camera, each server's earpiece, mapping the surveillance network with practiced efficiency. His fingers absently brushed the expensive watch on his wrist—not just a timepiece, she'd learn later, but one of many custom tools that helped maintain his cover. He caught Destiny's stare as he approached the table. Held it. A faint, challenging smirk touched his lips. He pulled out the chair directly opposite her and sat down, radiating an easy arrogance that felt... calculated.

"Destiny Rivers," he said, his voice a smooth baritone with a subtle, unplaceable accent. "Heard you cleaned Novo out in Vegas. Impressive." He extended a hand across the felt. "Rubben Kane.

Predictive analytics and cybersecurity. My specialty is finding patterns others miss."

Destiny hesitated for a fraction of a second, the memory of Shark's warning screaming in her head. His hand was waiting. Not taking it would be a tell, a sign of weakness or fear. She reached out. His grip was warm but calloused. Not the smooth hand of a tech millionaire who spent his days coding or managing portfolios. She filed away the discrepancy. "Mr. Kane. Heard you made a fortune in predictive analytics. Also impressive." She infused the words with just a hint of skepticism.

His smirk widened, acknowledging the unspoken challenge. "Flattery will get you everywhere, Ms. Rivers. Let's see if it gets me your chips." He released her hand, sending a surge of electricity up her arm. She filed it away as another potential threat.

The game began. Harrison dealt the first hand himself. The blinds started at $100,000. Ben was a wreck. Every bet made him flinch. His tells were glaringly obvious – a lip bite when he bluffed, a slight dilation of his pupils when he had a strong hand. He kept glancing towards Harrison, a look of terrified appeal. Then his gaze shifted to Destiny, lingering on her emerald earrings. Ben had seen them before. Celeste monitored the game on her tablet, occasionally murmuring something to Harrison.

Rubben played with a deceptive nonchalance. He chatted easily, projecting the image of the charming amateur riding his luck. But Destiny saw the sharp intelligence behind the facade, the way his eyes missed nothing, the subtle tightening of his jaw when he calculated odds. He was good. Playing a role, just like she was. His hands handled the chips with practiced ease.

Harrison played sparingly at first, more an observer than a participant. When he did enter a pot, it was with calculated aggression, his massive bets forcing folds or extracting maximum value. His tells were minimal, buried deep beneath layers of control. But Destiny caught it – the faintest tightening of the skin around his eyes when he was truly confident.. He wasn't just playing to win money. He was playing to dominate.

Hours in, Destiny caught pocket queens. The flop: Queen-Seven-Two. She checked, feigning weakness. Ben, clutching at straws, bet aggressively. Rubben called, his expression unreadable. Harrison, who had been quietly watching, reraised significantly. Ben folded, looking sick. Destiny paused, letting the tension build. She noticed the micro-tension in Rubben's shoulders, the way his thumb tapped once, against the table edge. He was strong, but not invincible. Harrison's face was a mask, but she caught that slight tightening around his eyes again.

She pushed all her remaining chips forward. "All in."

Silence descended. The clatter of chips ceased. Every eye at the table was fixed on her. Rubben leaned back in his chair. A slow smile spread across his face. "Bold move, Rivers. Very bold." He studied her. Destiny could feel Harrison's eyes boring into the side of her head. Rubben's smile didn't waver. He glanced at his cards again, then back at her. Then, with a sigh, he flipped his cards face down. "Too rich for my blood." He slid his cards towards the dealer. "Fold."

He'd folded too easily. Had he seen through her? Or was he playing a longer game? Harrison's expression didn't change, but the skin around his eyes tightened. He flipped his own cards – Ace-King. He'd been bluffing with nothing but high cards. Destiny turned over her queens, claiming the massive pot. A murmur ran through the onlookers. Harrison gave a slow, deliberate nod.

"Yuh have nerve, Ms. Rivers, real nerve." His voice was deep, smooth, the faint Jamaican lilt giving it a deceptive warmth.

The game continued, but the atmosphere shifted. Ben was drowning. He made increasingly desperate, foolish bets, his stack dwindling to nothing. Finally, he pushed his last meager chips into the center on a hopeless hand of Jack-high. Harrison called with a pair of threes. Ben lost. He slumped back in his chair. He looked like a man who'd just been handed a death sentence.

Celeste stood, her movements smooth and silent. "Mr. Wicker," she announced, her voice clear and devoid of inflection. "You have been eliminated from the tournament."

Ben looked around the table, eyes wide with terror. No one met his gaze except Destiny, and she couldn't help him. Harrison nodded, his expression one of mild disappointment. Two of the crew members, the ones Destiny had noted earlier with the telltale bulges beneath their jackets, materialized from the shadows near the entrance. They moved with silent, predatory grace.

"Please accompany us to your cabin, sir," one of them said, his voice flat, devoid of emotion. His hand rested lightly on Ben's shoulder.

Ben flinched violently. "No... please... I can... I have more money! I can wire it!" His voice cracked, rising in pitch.

Harrison's eyes she flickered towards him, a flicker of cold impatience. "Cease the noise, man. Your time done" He made a small, dismissive gesture with his hand.

The crew member's grip tightened. "This way, sir." It wasn't a request.

Ben stumbled to his feet, his legs seeming barely able to support him. He cast one last look around the table – a look of pure, animal terror. His eyes met Destiny's. In that instant, she saw it all: the knowledge of his own doom, the plea for an intervention that would never come. Then the guards steered him firmly towards the exit. The heavy doors swung shut behind them with a soft click.

The silence in the salon was absolute. The clink of a chip as Harrison stacked his winnings sounded unnaturally loud. He looked around the table, his smile returning. "Well. Shall we continue?"

Destiny stared at the closed doors, the image of Ben Wicker's terrified eyes burned onto her retina. The opulent room, the glittering table, the vast pot of chips in front of her – it all felt suddenly grotesque, a thin veneer over something monstrous. The cold dread that had settled in her stomach since boarding the *Royal Meridian* surged. She just knew that Ben wasn't being escorted to his cabin. He was being escorted to his grave. And she was next in line. The game wasn't just about money. It was about survival. She was trapped on a floating tomb with nowhere to run.

Chapter 3 - The Game Beneath the Game

Coffee and cigar smoke still lingered in the grand salon's stale air. Destiny stacked her chips with forced calm. The substantial pile formed a fortress wall built on Harrison's bluff and her own nerve.

The break was announced. Players dispersed, murmuring in low tones. Destiny moved with them, her steps unhurried, her face a study in detached composure. Inside, her mind raced. She needed proof of what they all suspected but dared not voice. Proof that this wasn't just high-stakes poker. It was an execution chamber.

In her cabin, Destiny retrieved the satellite phone she'd concealed in the lining of her suitcase. A precaution that now seemed prescient. She powered it on, the small screen glowing to life, then immediately flashing a 'NO SIGNAL' warning. She moved to the window, then the bathroom, then tried pressing it directly against the glass. Nothing. Not even a flicker of connectivity.

She wasn't surprised, not after seeing the communications center earlier. Harrison would have every frequency jammed, every satellite connection blocked. The yacht might as well be on another planet. No signals in. No signals out. Perfect isolation.

When Destiny came out of her room she drifted towards the service corridor near the kitchens, a zone of efficiency compared to the salon's oppressive glamour. The air here smelled of lemon disinfectant and something faintly greasy. She was about to follow when a soft click of heels made her freeze. Celeste appeared at the corridor junction, her tablet clutched against her chest rather than held casually at her side. Her eyes widened slightly at the sight of Destiny standing near the restricted area. For a tense moment, they stared at each other. Destiny braced for alarm, for guards to be called. Instead, Celeste glanced both ways down the corridor, then stepped closer.

"You shouldn't be here," she said, her voice barely above a whisper. "The service areas are monitored." She reached past Destiny, tapping a small, nearly invisible camera in the corner. Her eyes held Destiny's for a beat longer than necessary. "Some things, once seen, can't be unseen." She adjusted her tablet, revealing just enough of the screen for Destiny to glimpse what looked like security footage—the same laundry cart, the same bloodied shirt, being carefully documented. Then the tablet was turned away, the moment gone.

"Return to the salon, Ms. Rivers," Celeste said, her professional mask back in place. "Mr. Harrison doesn't appreciate guests wandering unescorted." The warning in her voice could have been interpreted multiple ways.

"Ladies and gentlemen," Celeste's voice cut through the murmur of conversation as players returned from the break. "We are entering level three of our tournament. Blinds will increase to $250,000/$500,000. Currently, twelve players remain." Her tablet displayed the updated standings on the salon's screens. "The top eight chip stacks are as follows."

Destiny noted her position—fourth, behind Harrison, Rubben, and a silent Japanese businessman she'd been carefully avoiding. Alex was in tenth position, his stack dwindling. The tournament structure was working as designed, pressuring the short stacks to make desperate moves or slowly bleed out to the blinds. Two more eliminations and they'd reach the halfway point. By tomorrow afternoon, they'd be down to the final table of five.

And then what? Destiny wondered. What happened to the survivors after Harrison had his entertainment?

When play resumed, every hand became an exercise in survival. Destiny played mechanically, her mind only partially on the cards. She folded strong hands, called with marginal ones. Her decisions were erratic enough to draw a raised eyebrow from Rubben across the table. He watched her, his green eyes sharp. She avoided his gaze, concentrating on the chips and on the microscopic tremble in Harrison's thumb as he pushed a stack forward. Survival required information. She needed to know what this ship was truly carrying besides doomed millionaires.

Destiny found herself studying Rubben Kane during the break. He stood near the bar, seemingly relaxed, but she caught the way his eyes tracked every crew member, every exit. Amateur tech millionaire? Not likely. His situational awareness was too sharp, too practiced.

Their eyes met across the salon. Instead of looking away, he raised his glass in a small salute. The gesture was both acknowledgment and challenge. She felt a small thrill of recognition—here was someone else who saw the game beneath the game.

When he approached her table during the dealing break, she was ready.

"Impressive read on Harrison's bluff," he said, his voice pitched low enough that only she could hear. "Not many people would have pushed back against him like that."

"You folded," she pointed out.

"I folded because you had it." His smile was different now—less performed, more genuine. "And because watching you work was more valuable than winning that particular hand."

The comment could have been condescending. Instead, it felt like professional respect. From one predator acknowledging another.

"Careful, Mr. Kane," she said, stacking her chips with deliberate precision. "Flattery might make me think you're trying to distract me."

"Would it work?"

She looked up, meeting his eyes directly. "No."

His smile widened. "Good. I'd hate to be disappointed."

As he walked away, Destiny realized she was looking forward to their next conversation. Dangerous territory. But then again, everything on this boat was dangerous territory.

During another break, Destiny feigned a need for the restroom, slipping away from the main flow of players and heading towards the lounge. The corridor was empty. A discreet 'Crew Only' sign pointed down a narrower passageway, lit with harsher fluorescent lights. Her pulse accelerated. This was reckless. Suicidal. But the image of the bloody shirt fueled her, overriding caution. She moved quickly, her boxer's training keeping her steps light, her senses hyper-alert.

The passage led to a heavy, unmarked metal door. It was slightly ajar. Destiny peered through the crack. Beyond lay a different world. Stark white walls, gray linoleum flooring, banks of monitors glowing with schematics and camera feeds showing different parts of the yacht. A communications hub. Two crew members sat at consoles, headsets on, speaking in low, clipped tones. Military jargon. Coordinates. And then, clear as a bell:

"...confirming rendezvous timeline. Cargo transfer confirmed for 2200. Assets secured

Destiny's mind snapped the terms into place. Not poker chips. Something else. Weapons? Drugs? The sterile room, the disciplined postures, the cold efficiency – it screamed paramilitary operation. This yacht wasn't just a venue; it was a mobile command center. Harrison's empire ran much deeper than she'd ever imagined. The poker tournament was a front, a gaudy distraction masking something far more lethal. She was trapped on a warship disguised as a pleasure cruiser.

Destiny turned down another corridor, following the mental map she was building of the yacht. She paused at a heavy door marked "Engineering - Authorized Personnel Only." As she studied the security panel beside it, she noticed it was an advanced model—biometric scanner, keypad, and what appeared to be an RFID reader. Fresh installation marks showed around the frame; the security system was newly upgraded.

A footstep echoed in the passage behind her. Destiny melted back into the shadows beside a utility closet, pressing herself flat against the metal wall. Footsteps approached. A crew member pushed through the heavy door into the comms hub. The door swung shut with a clang.

Rubben stood there on the deck, watching the endless ocean. The mission parameters had been clear three years ago when he'd begun infiltrating Harrison's organization. Build cover. Gain trust. Gather evidence of arms trafficking. But lately, Mia's communications had become increasingly problematic. Vague directives. Changed protocols without explanation. Resources that never materialized. And now, radio silence on extraction plans despite his repeated requests.

Standard operating procedure was clear: a field agent deep undercover always had primary, secondary, and emergency extraction plans in place before any high-risk operation. Yet Mia had been evasive for weeks, deflecting his questions with platitudes about "flexible response protocols" and "evolving tactical situations." It wasn't like her. It wasn't like the DEA.

Something was off. But after three years embedded, with the arms deal just days away, he couldn't afford to second-guess his handler. Still, the unease lingered, a shadow at the edges of his mind.

Destiny walked up beside him, leaving a careful six feet of polished deck between them. Close enough to talk. Far enough to run. The salt air was cool against her skin, but it did nothing to calm the unease he provoked in her.

"Predictive analytics," she said, her voice level. It wasn't a question.

He didn't turn immediately. A faint smile touched his lips. "Profitable field. Pays for the view." He gestured vaguely at the sunset.

"It pays for tailored suits," Destiny countered, her gaze fixed on his profile. "But it doesn't put callouses like that on a man's hands." She nodded towards his fingers, resting on the railing. The knuckles were lightly scarred, the skin thick and roughened. "Not unless you moonlight as a blacksmith. Or maybe... something that requires more dexterity than typing on a keyboard?"

Rubben finally turned to face her fully. The fading light caught the green in his eyes, turning them opaque, unreadable. The easy charm was gone, replaced by a watchful stillness that reminded her of a predator assessing a rival, not prey. "Observant, Ms. Rivers. I dabble in restoration. Antique clocks, mostly. Complicated mechanisms." His tone was smooth, but the explanation felt flimsy, tossed out like bait.

"Clocks," Destiny repeated, a hint of dry skepticism in her voice. "That must be why you fold a winning hand just to watch another player." She was referring to a pot they'd both been in an hour earlier, one he'd dropped out of for no logical reason. "Your timing is... unconventional."

Something flickered in his eyes—not surprise, but respect. A slow smile spread across his face, different from the one at the poker table. Less performed, more genuine. "Watching you work was more valuable than winning that particular pot. You don't just see the cards, you see the story behind them. It's fascinating."

The comment could have been a line. Instead, it felt like professional recognition. From one player acknowledging another. The pull she'd felt earlier intensified, a dangerous lure.

"Careful, Mr. Kane," she said, her voice soft but firm. "Flattery might make me think you're trying to distract me."

"Would it work?" he asked, stepping a little closer, the gap between them shrinking.

She looked up, meeting his eyes directly, the salty wind whipping a strand of hair across her face. "No."

His smile widened, a flash of white in the growing dusk. "Good. I'd hate to be disappointed." The admission hung between them. Professional respect, maybe. Or the recognition of a fellow survivor. Destiny felt something shift in her assessment of him—not trust, not yet, but a recalibration. He wasn't just another mark. He was the tell she couldn't yet read, and that made him the most dangerous person on the boat.

"Rivers."

Shark's voice cut through the salt air. He emerged from the shadows near the deck access, his face ashen, eyes darting between her and Rubben. He clutched a half-empty tumbler of whiskey.

Rubben's expression shifted instantly, becoming unreadable. Professional. He gave Destiny a single, meaningful look—*we'll finish this later*—before stepping back. "I'll leave you to your conversation."

Destiny watched him go, surprised by the small flicker of disappointment in her chest. Not frustration—something else. The sense of an important conversation left unfinished. She turned to Shark. "What is it?"

Shark ignored Rubben completely, his haunted eyes fixed on Destiny. He grabbed her arm, his grip surprisingly strong despite the tremors. "You need to come now. Please."He pulled her away from the railing, towards the relative shelter of a lifeboat davit.

Shark shoved her into the shadow of the davit winch. The smell of salt and grease was thick. He scanned the deck frantically, then leaned in close, his breath sour with whiskey and fear. Shark leaned toward Destiny, his bloodshot eyes darting nervously to ensure no one was listening.

"You're playing too conservatively," he muttered. "Tournament structure like this, with blinds escalating every ninety minutes, you can't afford to wait for premium hands."

Destiny had studied the board displayed on the big screen. The elimination schedule showed they'd reach the final table by tomorrow evening.

"I know how tournaments work," she replied quietly.

"Not this one," Shark whispered, a tremor in his voice. "You think this is about the prize money? Harrison's built the structure deliberately. Final hand concluding precisely at 2200 hours. You think that's coincidence?"

Destiny felt a chill. The tournament timeline matched exactly with what she'd overheard about the "delivery" in the communications hub. Whatever was happening tomorrow night at 10 PM, Harrison wanted most of the players eliminated by then, with only the final hand left to play. A spectacle to distract from something else entirely.

Chapter 4 - The Agent's Truth

Rubben's cabin on was a study in calculated anonymity. Like every other suite, it offered luxury – pale linen, teak accents, a bed wide enough to get lost in. But unlike the others, it held secrets. He sat at the sleek writing desk, the surface clear except for a thin, matte-black tablet.

First, he activated the signal jammer disguised as a wireless phone charger, creating a sphere of electronic white noise around the room. Then he used a compact frequency scanner hidden in his watch to sweep for bugs, methodically checking each corner. Only when he was certain did he press his thumb to a specific corner of the tablet. A biometric reader glowed faintly green beneath his skin, and the tablet's surface shimmered, resolving into a secure communications interface. The face that appeared was familiar: Agent Mia Young, his handler. Her dark hair was pulled back severely, emphasizing the sharp angles of her face and the dark smudges of fatigue beneath her eyes. The sterile glow of the DEA operations center backlit her.

"Rabbit," she greeted him, using his operational callsign. Her voice, stripped of warmth by encryption, was tight. "Status?"

"Stable, for now," Rubben replied, his own voice low, controlled. He kept his gaze fixed on the screen, his posture relaxed but alert, a practiced deception even in private. "Tournament continues. Harrison plays the gracious host, but the pressure's building. Another player eliminated tonight." He didn't specify Ben's fate. Mia didn't need the gory details. She needed actionable intelligence.

"Understood." Mia's eyes narrowed. "We've intercepted chatter, Rabbit. The timeline's accelerating. 'Delivery' is confirmed for Sector Seven tomorrow, 2200 local. We need concrete evidence *before* that happens. Photographs, manifests, anything that sticks Harrison to the cargo."

Rubben's jaw tightened. Operations always accelerated this way. Three years of meticulous infiltration, and now Harrison's greed had compressed everything into a frantic scramble. He thought of Destiny, her suspicion already pricking at his carefully constructed facade.

"I saw the cargo," he said flatly. "Secondary hold. Temperature-controlled crates, military-grade handling protocols. Surface-to-air missile launchers with the markings partially scraped off. Harrison isn't just moving handguns—he's arming militias."

The image flashed in his mind: two crew members maneuvering a long, narrow crate with the kind of reverence usually reserved for nuclear waste. He'd caught the stenciled outline partially scraped away but unmistakable – the silhouette of a surface-to-air missile launcher. This wasn't just smuggling handguns; it was arming militias, fueling wars.

Mia leaned in. "That's exactly what we need. Get inside that hold. Document everything. Harrison walks without hard evidence—he's too insulated." Her voice hardened. "This is the pivot point. We move now, or we lose him. And Rabbit... watch your six. If they're spooked..."

What about extraction?" Rubben asked, his voice low. "The window's closing fast. We need to finalize the protocol."

Mia's eyes shifted away from the camera momentarily. "Extraction is... complicated. Focus on the evidence first. We'll... figure out the details once you have what we need."

"That's not protocol," Rubben pressed. "Mia, I need firm extraction parameters. This is the third time you've deflected."

"Protocols change, Rabbit," she said, her voice hardening. "Get the evidence. That's the priority." Her expression softened artificially. "Trust the process. You're doing good work."

The evasion was becoming a pattern. A warning bell sounded distantly in Rubben's mind, but he pushed it aside. Three years in, he couldn't afford doubt.

"There's something else," he said, watching her reaction carefully. "Marcus Rivers' daughter is here. Destiny."

Mia's composure slipped for a microsecond—surprise, quickly masked by professional interest. "Rivers had a daughter? That's... unexpected. Is she involved in the operation?"

"No. She's a player. Professional poker." He deliberately withheld his suspicions about Harrison's interest in her. "But her presence complicates things."

"Stay focused, Rabbit," Mia replied. "She's not your concern. The evidence is all that matters. Rabbit out" The dismissal was too sharp, too absolute. Another red flag.

Mia's image dissolved, replaced by the tablet's black surface. The connection severed, leaving Rubben alone in the luxurious silence. The weight of the mission settled back onto his shoulders, heavier now. Accelerating timelines meant less room for error, less time to shield Destiny from the incoming storm. He had to get into that hold. Tonight.

He stood, moving to the porthole where the night ocean slid past. Destiny's face materialized in his mind—her fierce intelligence, her determination, that flash of vulnerability he'd glimpsed on the deck. He pressed his forehead to the cool glass. This wasn't in any operational manual. Sentiment was a liability, attraction a catastrophic risk. Every DEA field agent knew the rules. Yet each time she looked at him with those penetrating eyes, something shifted inside him, like tectonic plates shifting beneath his carefully constructed foundation. He was leading her into darkness, using her as an unwitting asset while Harrison's operation accelerated around them both. The thought left a bitter taste in his mouth.

"Focus," he muttered to his reflection. "The mission is what matters." But even as he straightened his tie and prepared to return to the game, he knew he was lying to himself. Destiny mattered too. And that truth terrified him more than any of Harrison's enforcers ever could.

After securing his tablet, Rubben checked his appearance in the mirror and headed for the poker room. The transition to the grand salon was jarring. The air thickened with the cloying scent of expensive cigars and spilled liquor. The vast oval poker table was an island of intense focus under the spotlight glare, surrounded by deepening shadows where observers lingered like ghosts. Rubben took his seat, his arrival noted by Harrison's sharp, assessing glance from the head of the table. Celeste sat nearby, her tablet glowing softly.

Destiny sat across the table, her posture rigidly controlled. But Rubben saw the tension in the line of her jaw, the almost tremor in the fingers resting on her stack of chips. She'd seen Ben taken away. She knew. She was seeing too much, too fast. It terrified him for her.

Then his focus shifted to the carnage unfolding at the table. Alex was disintegrating before their eyes. Sweat plastered his thinning hair to his forehead. His expensive shirt was damp under the arms. His hands fluttered over his dwindling stack of chips like panicked birds. Every bet he made was, a desperate prayer. Harrison, opposite him, watched with the fascination of a biologist observing a pinned insect. It wasn't cruelty driving him, but something colder—a businessman meticulously eliminating inefficiency. For Harrison, Alex was simply a faulty investment being written off the books. He played Alex not with overt aggression, but with a slow, relentless pressure that was infinitely more cruel. He'd fold strong hands when Alex showed weakness, letting him win a small pot, feeding the flicker of hope. Then, when Alex tentatively pushed chips forward on a mediocre hand, Harrison would pounce with a massive re-raise, forcing a fold or extracting maximum pain.

"Call," Alex croaked, pushing a stack of chips forward with trembling hands. He held a pair of eights. The flop had shown Queen, Ten, Four.

Harrison didn't even glance at his cards, steepling his fingers, his massive frame radiating cold power. His dark eyes fixed on Alex. "That's a significant bet, Mr. Morrison." His voice was a low rumble, making it sound almost conversational. "Significant for your current... position." He let the implication hang – Alex's stack was hemorrhaging. "Are you sure you want to commit so much on middle pair?" He tilted his head slightly, a predator feigning curiosity. "Perhaps you caught a glimpse of something? A tell? Or perhaps you're simply hoping I'm bluffing?"

Alex flinched as if struck. He licked his lips, a nervous tic Rubben had cataloged hours ago. "I... I call," Alex repeated, his voice cracking.

Harrison sighed theatrically, a sound of profound disappointment. He flipped his cards. Ace-Queen. Top pair. Alex's face crumpled. He stared at his eights like they'd betrayed him. Harrison reached forward, his movements deliberate, and raked in the pot. Alex's stack was reduced to a pitiful handful of high-denomination chips.

"All in," Alex whispered a few hands later, his voice a broken rasp. He pushed his last three chips forward. He held King-Jack offsuit. A prayer, not a hand.

Harrison studied him for a long moment. The silence stretched, thick and suffocating. Rubben saw Destiny tense, her knuckles where she gripped the edge of the table. Celeste tapped something into her tablet, her face impassive. Harrison finally nodded. "Call." He turned over... Ace-high. Nothing. A pure, cold-blooded bluff, called with nothing but the absolute certainty of Alex's terror. Alex turned over his King-Jack, a strangled sound escaping his throat as Harrison's high card won the pot.

Celeste stood, the movement smooth and silent as a shark's fin cutting water. "Mr. Morrison," she announced, her voice devoid of inflection, cutting through the stunned silence. "You have been eliminated from the tournament."

Alex didn't slump. He froze.

His eyes, wide with pure, unadulterated terror, locked onto Harrison's face. "Please..." The word was a dry rasp, barely audible. "Mr. Harrison... I... I have resources. Back home. I can get more money. A transfer... please..." He was begging, his voice rising in pitch, cracking with desperation. "Don't... please don't..."

Harrison regarded him with an expression of faint distaste, like a man finding a cockroach in his caviar. "The rules are explicit, Mr. Morrison. Elimination is final. Your participation is concluded." He made a minute gesture with one hand, a flick of dismissal.

Two crew members materialized from the shadows near the salon entrance. They moved with the silent, predatory grace Rubben associated with special forces washouts. One placed a large hand on Alex's shoulder. It wasn't violent, but the weight and intent behind it were undeniable. "This way, sir."

Alex flinched, a choked sob escaping him. He looked around the table, his eyes wild, pleading. They swept over Destiny, wide with a silent, desperate appeal that made Rubben's gut clench. Rubben saw the raw empathy, the fury, the helplessness warring in her eyes before she looked sharply away, her jaw set. The guards steered Alex firmly towards the exit. He stumbled, his legs seeming to buckle.

The heavy salon doors swung shut behind them with a soft, final click that echoed in the sudden silence.

The game resumed, a murmur of forced conversation breaking out. Harrison stacked his newly won chips. Rubben forced himself to breathe, to appear engrossed in his own cards. But his mind was racing. Alex wasn't a hardened criminal; he was a terrified kid in over his head. His execution was imminent. Rubben's training screamed *observe, document, maintain cover*. His conscience screamed *intervene*. And beneath both, a colder, more pragmatic voice whispered: *He knows something. He was asking questions. What did he find?*

Rubben waited two hands. Folded both early, projecting disinterest. Then he excused himself quietly, citing the need for air. He moved with deliberate casualness towards the exit, nodding politely to another player. Once in the corridor, the atmosphere shifted. The salon's oppressive tension gave way to the yacht's constant, low thrum. He turned not towards the outer decks, but deeper into the ship's belly, following the route he'd mentally mapped earlier, the route he'd seen the guards take Alex.

The service corridors were utilitarian, lit by harsh fluorescents that buzzed faintly. Rubben moved silently, a shadow among shadows, his senses hyper-alert. He rounded a corner and froze. Fifty feet ahead, Destiny was pressed against the wall beside a recessed maintenance alcove, her body coiled with tension. She was watching something inside. Before Rubben could pull her back, he heard it—a low groan, then the sickening, meaty thud of a fist hitting flesh.

He was on her in three silent strides, his hand closing over her arm just as she tensed to spring forward. She flinched, spinning on him, her eyes blazing with fury. He put a single finger to his lips, his gaze intense, commanding silence. He peered past her into the alcove.

Two of Harrison's guards stood over Alex. He was on his knees, his face already a bloody ruin. One guard held him by the hair while the other methodically beat him.

"Who told you to poke around, pretty boy?" the guard growled, flexing his knuckles.

Destiny tried to pull free from Rubben's grip, a low snarl in her throat. He held fast, his eyes never leaving the guards. He knew that a verbal bluff wouldn't work. His mission parameters had just changed from observation to survival. And Destiny was now part of that equation.

He released her arm, pushing her back against the wall. "Stay," he mouthed, the order absolute. Before she could protest, he moved.

Training overrode thought. He flowed from the shadows, not as a tech millionaire, but as the Ranger he used to be. The guard holding Alex's hair never saw him coming. Rubben's forearm slid under the man's chin in a perfect chokehold, lifting him off his feet and cutting off his air. The guard's hands clawed uselessly at Rubben's arm as his eyes bulged, his body going limp in seconds. Rubben let him drop, an unconscious heap on the floor.

The second guard spun, his face a mask of shock, his hand fumbling for the weapon at his hip. Rubben was already there. His hand shot out, not for the gun, but for the man's wrist, twisting it at an unnatural angle with a sharp crack of bone. The guard screamed—a sound that was cut short as Rubben's other hand, fingers rigid, delivered a sharp, precise strike to the side of the neck.

The man's eyes rolled back and he collapsed like a puppet with its strings cut.

The entire confrontation lasted less than ten seconds.

The silence that followed was absolute, broken only by Alex's ragged, wet gasps. Destiny stared, her mind a cold engine of analysis processing the brutal efficiency she had just witnessed. The charming amateur from the poker table was a fiction. This lethal predator was the truth. She filed it away. Another variable. Another piece of data on the man bleeding at her feet.

She pushed past Rubben and dropped to her knees beside Alex, her hands hovering, not knowing where to touch. "Alex? It's me, Destiny."

He coughed, blood flecking his lips. His one functioning eye fluttered open, struggling to focus on her face. "Your... father..."

Destiny froze, her spine visibly stiffening. "What about my father?"

Rubben knelt beside them, his eyes scanning the corridor, his senses on high alert. He began unceremoniously checking the guards' pockets for keys or comms devices.

Alex stirred. His one functioning eye fluttered open, unfocused at first, then locking onto Destiny's face hovering above him. Recognition flickered through the pain and confusion. His lips moved, forming soundless words. Destiny leaned closer, her ear almost touching his bloody lips. "Alex? What is it? Who did this?"

Alex coughed, a wet, bubbling sound. Blood flecked his lips. He strained, his body trembling with the effort. His voice was a shredded whisper, barely audible over the hum of the ship. "Your... father..."

Destiny froze, her spine visibly stiffening, breath catching in her throat. Rubben's blood turned to ice. *No. Not like this.*

"I was there," Alex rasped. "Harrison used... company funds for... weapons deals." His fingers weakly clutched at her sleeve. "Marcus found out... was going..."

Alex's eye rolled, struggling to focus. He gasped, drawing in a ragged breath that rattled in his chest. "...Harrison..." The name was a bloody exhale. "...killed him..." His voice faded, the last word a mere exhale. "...run..."

Alex's body shuddered one last time, a final, rattling breath escaping his lips. He was gone.

For a moment, there was nothing but the hum of the ship. Then Rubben's voice, low and urgent, cut through her shock. "Help me."

She looked up, her eyes vacant. Rubben was already dragging the first unconscious guard towards a large electrical maintenance closet set into the far wall. The message was clear: Accomplice or liability. There was no third option.

The choice was automatic. She grabbed the second guard under the arms, the dead weight a shock to her system. Together, they shoved the unconscious bodies into the cramped space, the door hissing shut with a heavy clang. They were now bound by more than a hunch. They were coconspirators.

Chapter 5 - Death of a Legend

She clamped a hand over her mouth, her eyes burning not with sadness but pure fury. She wanted to tear Harrison apart with her bare hands. What had her father been involved in that got him killed?

She stared at the lifeless form. Alex was gone. Another casualty of Harrison's empire. Another loose end tied up. Her father's face superimposed itself over Alex's ruined features. The grief, held at bay by fury, surged forward, a tidal wave threatening to drown her. She squeezed her eyes shut, fighting it back. Grief was a luxury she couldn't afford. Not here. Not now.

When she opened her eyes, Rubben was still there. That flicker of anguish was still there, raw and exposed for a split second before he shuttered it. But Destiny had seen it. Another tell in the endless game.

She pushed herself to her feet. She stepped over Alex's legs, closing the distance between her and Rubben. She stopped inches from him, forcing him to look down at her.

"You knew." It wasn't a question. It was an accusation, cold and absolute.

Rubben met her gaze. "Destiny..." he began, his voice rough.

"Don't." She cut him off, the single word sharp as shrapnel. "Don't say my name. Don't lie to me. Not again. How long have you known Harrison murdered my father?"

"I suspected," he said, his voice urgent. He glanced down the corridor. "But I didn't have proof. Not until... recently. Not until I was embedded here."

"Embedded?" Destiny echoed, the word tasting foreign, dangerous. Her analytical mind, struggling against the tide of emotion, latched onto it. "What does that mean? Who are you?"

Destiny saw the calculation flicker behind his eyes, the weighing of risks, the assessment of damage control. It fueled her fury. "Tell me the truth," she hissed, stepping even closer, invading his space deliberately. "Or I swear to God, I'll walk into that salon right now and tell Harrison exactly what Alex just told me, and exactly who I think you really are."

The threat hung in the air. Rubben's gaze locked onto hers with intensity. She saw the conflict warring within him. Finally, he exhaled. His shoulders slumped, not in surrender, but in the shedding of a colossal weight. When he spoke, his voice was stripped of all pretense.

"DEA." The word dropped between them like a stone. "My name is Rubben Kane. I'm an agent with the Drug Enforcement Administration. I've been undercover on this yacht for three weeks, investigating Harrison's arms trafficking operation. The poker tournament... it's a front. A distraction."

DEA. The letters echoed in the hollow space Alex's revelation had carved inside her. Undercover. Arms trafficking. The pieces smashed together with brutal clarity. The military bearing of the crew. The hidden comms hub. The 'delivery'. Sector Seven. It all made a horrifying, logical sense. And he'd known. He'd known about her father's connection. He'd used her. Played her. Just another piece on Harrison's board, manipulated by a different master.

The betrayal was sharp and deep. The corridor walls seemed to press in, the fluorescent lights buzzing like angry insects. She felt dizzy, nauseous. He was never restoring antiques. He was maintaining a fiction that had endangered her life the moment she stepped aboard.

"You used me," she whispered. "You sat there, knowing Harrison killed him, and you let me walk into this blind." The image of her father's smile contrasted violently with Rubben's masked face. "Was I part of your investigation? Am I just... leverage?"

"No!" He took a step toward her, his hand lifting then freezing mid-air. "Destiny, listen. I didn't know about your father's connection when I saw your name on the player list. Not for sure. It was a suspicion, a thread I was following. My priority was the arms deal. Getting evidence. Stopping Harrison. Telling you... it would have compromised the operation. Put you in even more danger." His eyes pleaded with her. They filled with a sincerity that felt like another layer of the lie. "I wanted to protect you."

"Protect me?" A harsh, brittle laugh escaped her. "By letting me bond with my father's killer over poker? What kind of protection is that?" She shook her head, the movement jerky. "You didn't protect Alex. You watched them drag him away. You stood there while they beat him to death for asking questions. Questions *I* should have been asking!" Her voice rose, fueled by the grief and fury churning inside her. "You're just like him! Using people. Playing games with lives!"

It's not a game!" The controlled agent vanished, replaced by raw intensity. "People are going to die tomorrow night if I don't stop that delivery! Hundreds, maybe thousands! This isn't just about your father—it's about surface-to-air missiles being handed to a cartel that shoots down civilian aircraft!" He stepped closer. "Yes, I lied. I used the tools I had because the stakes are that high. And yes, I knew about your father. I found the connection buried deep in old case files – Marcus Rivers, Harrison's original partner in the security firm that became... this. He found out what Harrison was planning, tried to back out, tried to expose him. Harrison had him eliminated. Made it look like an accident. I'm sorry, Destiny. God, I'm so sorry you had to find out like this. But I couldn't tell you. Not until I had proof. Not until it was safe."

Marcus Rivers, Harrison's original partner. The words unlocked a floodgate. Fragmented memories, suppressed for years, surged forward with horrifying clarity. Her father, packing a suitcase, his face grim, not excited. *Just a long business trip, sweetheart. Be good for Grandma.* The hushed, urgent phone calls late at night, the way he'd quickly hang up if she entered the room. Her grandmother's tight-lipped disapproval whenever his name was mentioned. *Your father... he keeps dangerous company.* And the silence after the 'accident'. The closed casket. The unanswered questions politely brushed aside. It hadn't been grief clouding her memory; it had been a child's instinctive repression of a truth too terrifying to face. Her father hadn't been a victim of random tragedy. He'd been a target. A casualty of the same monstrous enterprise she was now trapped within. Harrison hadn't just killed him; he'd stolen her childhood, her sense of safety, her very understanding of the world.

The grief hit her. She swayed, bracing a hand against the cold wall of the alcove. Her father hadn't abandoned her. He'd been taken. Murdered for trying to do the right thing. She squeezed her eyes shut, fighting the sob building in her chest. She couldn't break. Not here. Not in front of this DEA liar.

"Safe?" she managed, her voice thick. She opened her eyes, blinking back the hot sting. "Nothing is safe here. You brought me into this. Your operation... it's why I'm trapped on this boat with a killer." The accusation hung heavy. She saw the impact of it in the flicker of regret in his eyes. But it was replaced by a focused intensity.

"I didn't bring you here, Destiny," he said quietly. "You chose to come. You answered the invitation. But you're right. You *are* trapped. And so am I. Harrison suspects something. He's tightening security. Watching everyone." He glanced down the corridor again. "We need to move. Now. They'll come for the body soon."

Destiny looked down at her hands, sticky with Alex's blood. She wiped them frantically on her pants, leaving rusty smears. She looked back at Rubben. Trust was impossible. But survival...

survival demanded pragmatism. Hatred warred with a desperate need for his expertise.

Before she could respond, before she could decide if spitting in his face or begging for a plan was the wiser course, heavy footsteps echoed down the corridor. Rubben reacted instantly. He grabbed her arm with urgent force, pulling her away from the alcove, away from Alex's body, and into the deeper shadows of a recessed doorway across the hall. He pressed her back against the door, his body shielding hers from view, one hand clamped firmly over her mouth before she could make a sound. His other hand rested on the small of his back, beneath his jacket. Ready. His eyes, inches from hers in the dimness, held a silent, desperate command: *Stay. Still.*

The footsteps grew louder. Two figures rounded the corner—the same guards who had beaten Alex. They moved with grim efficiency, one spotting the alcove and gesturing silently to his partner. Destiny held her breath, pressed against Rubben's chest. The hard muscle beneath his shirt, the rapid beat of his heart against her back. His hand over her mouth was warm, firm. The scent of him mingled with blood and her own fear. His proximity: both violation and terrifying anchor.

The guards reached the alcove. One knelt, checking Alex's pulse with clinical disinterest. He shook his head. The other guard pulled a large, black body bag from a pouch on his belt. They worked swiftly, silently, rolling Alex's limp form into the bag, zipping it closed with a sound like a knife being drawn. They hefted the bag between them and turned, walking back the way they came, the burden swinging slightly between them. The footsteps faded.

Rubben didn't move immediately. He held her there, listening. Waiting until the silence was absolute except for the ship's hum and Destiny's own frantic heartbeat pounding in her ears. He lowered his hand from her mouth. He didn't step back. His gaze searched her face in the gloom, his eyes holding a question, a silent plea for understanding she couldn't possibly give.

The intercom crackled to life overhead which made them both flinch. Celeste's smooth voice echoed through the corridor: "All remaining tournament participants are requested to return to the Grand Salon immediately. Mr. Harrison has an important announcement."

Destiny pushed against Rubben's chest, breaking the contact. The warmth where his body had been pressed against hers vanished, replaced by a sudden chill. She straightened her shirt, avoiding his eyes, the phantom pressure of his hand still lingering on her lips. Alex was gone and they were being summoned back to the lion's den.

"We have to go," Rubben said quietly, his voice strained. He pocketed the signal disruptor, checking his watch. "Play along. Say nothing."

As they reached the door, the small device on his wrist vibrated once—a warning. He held up his hand, stopping Destiny before she could open the door. He pointed silently to his ear, then to the corridor beyond. Someone was waiting, listening.

Rubben raised his voice, transforming his tone to one of cold dismissal. "Consider yourself warned, Ms. Rivers. Your reckless accusations are not just unfounded, they're dangerous. I suggest you focus on the tournament instead of inventing conspiracy theories."

Understanding flashed in Destiny's eyes. She matched his performance instantly. "Just stay away from me, Kane. I don't trust you, and I never will."

She yanked open the door to find one of Harrison's security personnel "coincidentally" checking something on the wall panel nearby. The man straightened, his hand drifting toward the weapon concealed beneath his jacket. He looked between them, searching for signs of collusion.

"Problem?" the guard asked, his eyes cold.

"None at all," Rubben replied smoothly, brushing past. "Ms. Rivers was just making a rather theatrical exit from our conversation."

Destiny shot him a look of genuine loathing, only half-feigned. "Including you." She pushed past him, her back straight, her stride steady despite the tremor in her hands. Trust was the ultimate gamble, and Rubben had just shown her his hand was nothing but lies. Yet they were playing for the same pot now—survival.

Destiny's legs carried her on autopilot, away from Alex's blood soaking the knees of her trousers. Cabin. Change. Breathe. The words repeated like a metronome as she slipped into her suite and thumbed the biometric lock.

Inside, silence crashed over her. Shock wanted to drag her under, but habit shoved it aside. She stripped the ruined pants, wadding the fabric into a tight, guilty knot. Rust-brown stains had already stiffened the wool.. She stuffed the bundle into one of the suite's laundry pouches, vacuum-snapped it shut, then jammed the plastic brick beneath the false floor of her carry-on.

Mirror, sink, water scalding hot. Scarlet spirals disappeared down the drain while her pulse slammed against her throat. Alex's last words echoed—"...Harrison... killed..."—and for five lethal seconds she swayed, dizzy with grief and rage.

Focus, Rivers. Final table's still ahead.

She toweled off, yanked on the spare pair of black slacks, and slid her feet back into polished loafers. Fresh bruises bloomed purple along her ribs; she touched them, catalogued the pain, filed it under "Later."

At the door she paused, palm on the cold metal, whispering to the empty room, "Play the hand in front of you." Then she forced the mask into place and stepped into the corridor.

A s Destiny walked back to the main hall, from the upper deck she could see the ocean stretching endlessly in all directions. But it wasn't entirely empty. At the periphery of her vision, she spotted a sleek, gray vessel moving parallel to their course, maintaining a precise distance. Not close enough to be obvious, but there. Watching. A moment later, she caught sight of another, this one off the stern. Patrol boats, disguised as fishing vessels, but moving with military precision.

"Security detail," Rubben's voice came from behind her, pitched low enough that only she could hear. "There are four of them. They maintain a perimeter at all times. Armed with anti-personnel weapons and electronic countermeasures. If anyone tries to leave the yacht without authorization..." He didn't need to finish the thought.

The isolation wasn't just technological. It was enforced by guns and men willing to use them. Harrison had created a perfect prison in international waters, beyond the reach of any law enforcement. A floating black site where people disappeared and no one would ever know.

The salon felt different. The air, usually thick with tension and cigar smoke, now crackled with something more primal. The remaining players were gathered. The forced camaraderie was gone, replaced by a brittle silence. Shark Williams stood near the back, clutching a fresh drink. Celeste stood beside Harrison's empty chair as if at attention. Harrison himself stood near the panoramic windows overlooking the black ocean, his massive frame silhouetted against the vast void. He turned as Destiny and Rubben entered, his dark eyes sweeping over them, lingering on Destiny.

"Ah, Ms. Rivers. Mr. Kane." Harrison's voice carried effortlessly through the silent room. "Prompt. Excellent." He walked towards the poker table, but didn't sit. He stopped at the head, placing his massive hands flat on the polished wood. "It seems," he began, his tone almost regretful, "that the spirit of competition has... escalated beyond the boundaries of good sportsmanship. Earlier tonight, one of our fellow players, Mr. Alex Morrison, regrettably suffered a severe... medical episode. He has been taken to the infirmary for observation." A blatant, chilling lie delivered with absolute conviction. "However, his unfortunate situation is not the cause for this gathering."

He straightened, his gaze sweeping the room, pinning each player in turn. He continued, his voice hardening. "It has come to my attention that there is a snake among us." The word hissed through the silence. Destiny looked towards Rubben. He stood rigid beside her with a blank stare. Harrison's eyes didn't linger on him; they continued their relentless scan.

As Harrison surveyed the room, his gaze lingered on Destiny with an intensity that made her skin crawl. Not just the predatory assessment she'd seen before, but something more focused, calculating. As if he were looking through her, searching for something hidden. The emerald at her ear suddenly felt warm, her father's voice echoing in her memory: "Remember the patterns, Destiny. They're the key to everything." She'd always thought he meant card patterns. Now, she wasn't so sure.

Harrison continued. "Someone has violated the sanctity of this game. Someone attempted to cheat."

Harrison paused, letting the accusation sink in. Then he reached into his jacket pocket and removed a small silver device. "I believe in transparency. In evidence." He pressed a button, and a woman's voice filled the salon.

"Rabbit, the timeline's accelerating. 'Delivery' is confirmed for Sector Seven tomorrow, 2200 local. We need concrete evidence before that happens."

The recording continued, clear and clinical: "Get inside that hold. Document everything. Harrison walks without hard evidence—he's too insulated."

Harrison's eyes swept the room, lingering momentarily on Rubben. The message was unmistakable. Destiny felt her blood run cold as she recognized the voice from Rubben's earlier description—his handler, Mia Young.

"Fascinating, isn't it?" Harrison said, clicking off the device. "How easily loyalty can be purchased." His smile was glacial. "Federal agents should be more careful about who they trust."

He slipped the device back into his pocket. "Such actions constitute not only a breach of trust but a direct threat to the security of everyone aboard. Weakness and desperation are understandable flaws. But betrayal?" He shook his head slowly, a gesture of profound disappointment that was infinitely more terrifying than anger. "That is a cancer. And cancer must be eliminated."

He raised a hand. A side door opened. Two guards dragged in a man Destiny recognized – a quiet, middle-aged player named Theo, who kept mostly to himself. He looked dazed, terrified, his lip split, one eye swollen shut. They hauled him towards the center of the room, near the vast windows overlooking the endless black ocean.

"Mr. Theo," Harrison announced, his voice devoid of all inflection, "was discovered attempting to bypass security protocols near the primary communications array. He was searching for... what, Mr. Theo? An escape? A way to call for help?" He didn't wait for an answer Theo couldn't possibly give. "His actions have consequences. Consequences that affect us all."

Harrison walked towards the windows. He pressed a button on a sleek panel set into the wall. With a near-silent hum, a large section of the floor-to-ceiling glass panel began to retract sideways, vanishing into the wall. A rush of cool air flooded the salon. The void beyond the rail was absolute darkness. Harrison turned back to face the room, standing framed by the opening, the black ocean yawning behind him like a hungry mouth.

The rules of engagement have changed," Harrison declared, his voice cutting through the sudden gust of wind.

"Effective immediately, any attempt at cheating, espionage, or unauthorized access to restricted areas will be met with..."

He paused.

"Terminal disqualification."

He nodded towards the guards holding Theo. They didn't hesitate. With brutal efficiency, they hauled the struggling man towards the open window. Theo's cries were thin, terrified shrieks lost in the wind.

"No! Please! I didn't—!"

His words vanished as they lifted him over the low railing and shoved.

There was no splash.

No sound at all over the wind and the ship's engines.

One second Theo was there, screaming.

The next—gone.

Swallowed by the infinite blackness.

Harrison pressed the button again. The glass panel slid smoothly back into place, sealing the salon once more, shutting out the cold air and the horrifying emptiness beyond. The silence that followed was profound, suffocating. Players stared, frozen in shock and terror. Celeste looked down at her tablet, her face pale but composed. Shark had closed his eyes, his hand trembling around his glass.

Harrison surveyed the room, his expression calm, satisfied. He picked up a crystal tumbler of bourbon from a nearby table. He raised it in a mock toast.

"To clarity," he said, his voice smooth once more, the faint Jamaican lilt back in place. He took a slow sip, his dark eyes locking onto Rubben. "Di rat always expose himself. Always." He continued staring at Rubben as if it were a challenge. Then it swept dismissively over Destiny before moving on. The message was clear. He knew. And the game had just become a hunt.

Chapter 6 – Compromised

The word 'compromised' echoed in Rubben's skull as Harrison's announcement hung in the salon's silence. This wasn't suspicion. Harrison knew. Three years of meticulous infiltration, building trust thread by agonizing thread, sacrificed in an instant by the one person who was supposed to have his back. Agent Mia Young. His handler. His betrayer.

The silence following Theo's execution was broken by the soft tap of Celeste's heels as she approached the table, her face composed but noticeably paler. She cleared her throat.

"After this evening's... interruption, play will resume in thirty minutes," she announced, her voice steady despite the tremor in her hands. "We currently have seven players remaining. Tomorrow's final table will seat five. The current blind structure is \$500,000/\$1,000,000."

She touched her tablet, and the large screen updated with player standings. "The tournament will conclude tomorrow evening at

8 PM, coinciding with Mr. Harrison's gala celebration." Her eyes flickered briefly to the spot where the window had opened to the ocean. "The winner will receive their prize immediately following the conclusion of the final hand."

Destiny studied the schedule. The tournament's conclusion—8 PM tomorrow—aligned precisely with the weapons delivery Rubben had mentioned. 2200 hours. The timing wasn't coincidental. Harrison was planning to conclude both his business and his pleasure simultaneously.

Harrison's faint, satisfied smile as he surveyed the room was a knife twisting in the wound. He didn't look at Rubben directly, not yet. He was savoring the terror he'd unleashed, the paranoia crackling through the air like static. But Rubben felt the weight of his awareness. The game was up. The carefully constructed persona of Rubben Kane, tech entrepreneur and high-stakes amateur, was exposed—a marked man with nowhere to run.

The salon emptied quickly after Harrison's demonstration. Players retreated to their cabins, pale-faced and silent. Destiny lingered, watching as Harrison conferred quietly with Celeste. Even from a distance, the tension in their conversation was evident.

"Increase security protocols," Harrison ordered, his voice carrying just enough for Destiny to hear. "Full biometric lockdown on all restricted areas. Double the guards on the weapons shipment. No one accesses the cargo hold without my direct authorization." His eyes scanned the room, cold and calculating. "The DEA agent is still on board. Find them. Use whatever means necessary."

Celeste nodded, her fingers flying across her tablet. The yacht would become even more compartmentalized. Whatever freedom of movement had existed before was gone. She glanced towards the spot where Theo had been thrown into the void then followed Harrison to his quarters.

Harrison stood at the window of his private office, watching the endless black ocean scroll past. The room was dark except for the soft glow of monitors displaying surveillance feeds from throughout the yacht.

"The Rivers girl continues to use her father's betting patterns," Celeste said, breaking the silence. She stood just inside the doorway, tablet in hand, her silver dress gleaming in the dim light. "Our analysts are running them through the decryption software now."

Harrison didn't turn. "Marcus was clever. Embedding operational data into poker strategies he taught his daughter. A dead man's failsafe. Use the child as an unwitting courier of information that would only make sense to someone looking for it."

"And you're certain she doesn't know?" Celeste asked, her voice carefully neutral.

"Oh, she knows nothing." Harrison finally turned, his massive frame silhouetted against the darkness beyond. "Marcus would never have knowingly endangered his precious daughter. That's why her patterns are so pure, so unconscious. She has no idea she's been carrying the keys to her father's encrypted files for seventeen years."

His eyes gleamed in the monitor light. "By tomorrow night, we'll have extracted every last secret from her play. And then..." He let the sentence hang unfinished in the air between them.

Celeste's tablet trembled almost imperceptibly in her hand. "And then what, exactly?"

Harrison's smile widened. "And then we complete the Rivers family reunion. Permanently."

Rubben moved on autopilot, his training the only thing keeping his steps steady. Inside, his mind raced. Extraction was impossible. Communication was cut. Mia's betrayal meant the DEA wasn't coming; they were likely feeding Harrison intelligence right now. His official mission was dust. Survival was the only objective left. And survival meant Destiny Rivers.

He found her cabin door unlocked. A small, reckless defiance, or perhaps an invitation to the confrontation they both knew was coming. He slipped inside, closing the door behind him, engaging the deadbolt. The suite was dim, lit only by the ambient glow of the ocean through the panoramic window. Destiny stood silhouetted against the vast with her back to him. She hadn't changed her blood-smeared pants. The dark stains looked like inkblots in the low light. Her shoulders were rigid, her fingers gripped the windowsill until her knuckles whitened, her breath coming in controlled, measured intervals—the restraint of someone containing volcanic rage.

"Come to spin more lies, Agent Kane?" Her voice was arctic, cutting through the silence. She didn't turn around.

The title, delivered with that icy contempt, was another blow. He deserved it. He walked further into the room, stopping a few feet behind her.

"No more lies," Rubben said softly. He swept his hand along the edge of the desk, removing a small device from his pocket with practiced subtlety. He pressed something, and a soft, almost imperceptible hum filled the air. "Not to you. Not anymore."

What is that?" Destiny demanded.

"Signal disruptor," he explained quietly. "My cover as a tech entrepreneur specializing in cybersecurity isn't completely fabricated. It's given me access to custom surveillance countermeasures. This creates a bubble of electronic interference - messy enough to block listening devices, subtle enough to look like normal electromagnetic noise if they're scanning." He gestured to the small device. "We have about ten minutes before the pattern becomes suspicious. After that, we change locations."

"You've been doing this the whole time?" Destiny asked, the realization dawning.

"Every private conversation. Every coded message. It's a dance—create interference that looks like normal electronic noise, move before they can triangulate, never use the same location twice in succession." He ran a hand through his hair. "Harrison's surveillance network is extensive, but it has blind spots if you know where to look."

After a moment, Destiny shot back. "Why? Why keep it from me? My father... Harrison... you *knew*." Her voice broke on the last word, the raw grief beneath the fury momentarily surfacing. "You sat there, playing your little undercover game, while I bonded with his killer over fucking poker chips!"

The accusation was justified. Devastating. He met her furious gaze, refusing to look away. "I knew Harrison killed him. I didn't have absolute proof until I accessed encrypted files deep in Harrison's network a week before this tournament started." He paused, forcing the next words out, knowing they would wound her deeper. "Your father wasn't just Harrison's partner, Destiny. He was DEA. An informant."

The letters echoed in the hollow space Alex's revelation had carved inside her. DEA. It was an impossible variable inserted into a solved equation. The numbers didn't add up. Probability couldn't reconcile the man who taught her chess with a man who carried a gun for the government. But the other data points—the hushed phone calls, the 'business trips,' the closed casket—slammed into place with undeniable logic. It wasn't about the cards. It never had been. He hadn't been playing for money; he'd been playing for time. And his time had run out

"What?" The whisper was barely audible.

"Your father infiltrated Harrison's operation eight years ago," Rubben said, watching her face carefully. "He was gathering intel on weapons shipments, offshore accounts, the whole network."

Destiny gripped the edge of the window frame. "That's impossible. He was a security consultant. He—"

"Was one of our best," Rubben cut in. "He maintained his cover for nearly three years. Even his closest friends didn't know."

"My mother?"

Rubben shook his head. "For her protection. Same reason you were kept in the dark."

Destiny pressed her palm against her forehead. "The business trips. The late-night calls." Understanding dawned in her eyes. "The cash I found hidden in his desk drawer."

"Emergency funds," Rubben confirmed. "Standard protocol."

She turned back to the window, her reflection fragmented by the water's glare. "What happened?"

"He discovered Harrison's plan to sell surface-to-air missiles to a terror cell in Southeast Asia." Rubben's voice lowered. "He tried to extract himself, contacted his handler for an emergency pickup. Somehow, Harrison found out."

Destiny's shoulders tensed. "And made it look like an accident."

Destiny closed her eyes. A single tear traced a path through the dust and tension on her cheek. She turned away, one hand pressed against her mouth. Seconds stretched into a full minute as she stood motionless. When she opened her eyes again, the fury was still there, banked now, mixed with a dawning, horrifying understanding. "And you couldn't tell me," she stated, not a question. "Because the mission came first."

"Because telling you would have put a target on your back the size of this yacht," Rubben corrected, the frustration bleeding into his voice. "Harrison didn't know Marcus had a daughter. Certainly not one who could connect him to the past. If I'd told you and you reacted it would have drawn his attention. Would have put you in the crosshairs years ago. And once you were on this boat..." He shook his head. "Knowing would have gotten you killed faster. Like Alex."

"So you protected me by lying to me," Destiny said flatly. "By letting me walk into the lion's den blind." She pushed off the window frame, taking a step towards him. Raw grief still filled her eyes, but purpose now tempered it. "Your handler. Mia Young. She's the one who sold you out?"

The betrayal still felt raw, a wound too fresh to examine closely. Rubben nodded grimly. "The signs were there. I just refused to see them. Delayed responses. Withheld resources. Constantly evading questions about extraction protocols. Three years of my life, and she was playing me the whole time."

He raked a hand through his hair, frustration evident in every line of his body. "Two weeks ago, I requested emergency extraction after witnessing a test firing of the missiles. Standard procedure. She delayed, made excuses. Then yesterday, when I pressed about backup plans during the weapons transfer, she shut me down completely. 'Get the evidence first,' she said. No agent handler operates that way unless..."

"Unless they never intended for you to get out alive," Destiny finished, understanding dawning in her eyes.

"Harrison didn't just turn her," Rubben said, the realization still bitter on his tongue. "He's been using her to manipulate me, to control exactly what intelligence reaches the DEA. I've been an unwitting double agent, feeding sanitized information back to my own people while Harrison used me to misdirect their attention."

He met her gaze, laying his own cards on the table, the only ones he had left. "I'm not here as DEA anymore. I'm here as a man who needs to stop Harrison. And I need your help."

A harsh, brittle laugh escaped Destiny. "My help? You expect me to trust you now? After everything?"

"No," Rubben said honestly. "I don't expect trust. I'm asking for a tactical alliance. A shared objective: survival and bringing Harrison down." He gestured towards the door. "He just executed a player as a message. He knows there's a federal agent on board. He's locking this ship down. His tech team are elite former military and intelligence personnel. They operate a signal jamming dome that extends ten nautical miles in all directions. Every frequency, every band, every possible communication method is blocked or monitored."

He gestured toward the endless ocean outside. "We're approximately two hundred miles southeast of Miami, in a deliberate dead zone chosen to avoid shipping lanes and air traffic. The patrol boats maintain a constant perimeter. The yacht itself has anti-drone countermeasures and subsurface sensors to prevent underwater approach."

His eyes met hers, grim reality in every word. "This isn't just a boat, Destiny. It's a fortress designed specifically to ensure that nothing gets in or out without Harrison's explicit permission. That's why the DEA approved such a deep-cover operation. It's the only way to get close enough to gather evidence."

He saw the calculation in her eyes, the rapid assessment of odds, risks, and resources. Just like reading a poker table. Her gaze flickered to his hands, then back to his face. "What's the play?"

Relief warred with the grim reality. She was in. For now. "Harrison's weakness is his arrogance," Rubben said, lowering his voice further. "He thinks he's untouchable. He thinks he's broken everyone. But he hasn't. Celeste Montenegro."

Destiny's eyes narrowed. "She looked sick when Theo went overboard."

"Exactly. She's the operational brain. She runs the legitimate fronts, enjoys the luxury. But she's not a sadist. Harrison's escalating violence… it's destabilizing her. We saw it tonight. That's our leverage. That's our weak spot in his armor."

"How do we exploit it?" Destiny asked, her voice all business now. Her grief and fury crystallized into cold determination.

"We need to isolate her. Get her alone. Offer her a way out. Immunity. Protection. A chance to walk away from this before Harrison drags her down with him." Rubben paused. "But it has to be you. She won't trust me. Not now. You're another player, another victim in his game. Find a moment. Appeal to her self-preservation. Her disgust."

Destiny nodded slowly, absorbing the plan. "And what about Shark?"

"Broken. Terrified. Harrison owns him through debt. He's a liability, but potentially a useful distraction if we need one." Rubben's mind raced ahead. "The arms deal. The 'delivery'. It's happening tomorrow night. Surface-to-air missiles. Harrison's final move before consolidating power. The tournament finale coincides with it. That's our hard deadline. We stop the deal, we expose Harrison, or we die trying."

Before Destiny could respond, a sharp knock sounded on the cabin door. Not the polite tap of a steward. Authoritative. Rubben's hand instinctively went to the small of his back, beneath his jacket, fingers brushing the cool ceramic of his knife. Destiny tensed, her eyes locking with his.

"Ms. Rivers? Mr. Kane?" Celeste's voice, smooth and controlled, filtered through the door. "Mr. Harrison requests your presence in the salon. The final table commences in ten minutes."

"We'll be right there," Destiny called back, her voice remarkably steady.

Footsteps retreated down the corridor. The reprieve was over. The endgame had begun.

Destiny turned back to the window, staring out at the vast, empty ocean. The reflection in the glass showed her face – pale, set, the emerald at her ear a tiny, defiant spark in the darkness. "He invited me here, didn't he?" she asked quietly, the realization dawning with chilling certainty. "It wasn't random. He knew who I was. He wanted me here."

Rubben didn't need to confirm it. The pieces fit. Harrison eliminating the last loose end, the final ghost of Marcus Rivers. Turning her elimination into a twisted spectacle. "Yes," he said.

She turned to face him fully. The anger was still there, a banked fire in her dark eyes, but it was joined now by something else. A steely resolve. An acceptance of the brutal stakes. "Then let's make sure he regrets it."

She walked towards the door. Rubben moved to follow, but she paused, her hand on the knob. She looked back at him, not with the cold fury of before, but with a look that was complex. For a second, the mission, the crushing weight of the past and the terrifying uncertainty of the future all fell away. It was just them. Two damaged people, bound by betrayal and a shared enemy, standing on the precipice. Her gaze held his, a silent communication that bypassed words – acknowledgment of the truth, the fragile alliance, the terrifying odds.

Then it was gone. She opened the door, stepping out into the brightly lit corridor without a backward glance. Rubben took a breath. He followed her out, closing the cabin door softly behind him.

They were halfway to the salon when the voices reached them—two guards conversing in low tones around the corner ahead. Rubben's hand shot out, stopping Destiny. He pulled her into the shadow of a service alcove, pressing a finger to his lips.

"—moving the timeline up. Full lockdown protocols in thirty minutes." The first voice was clipped, professional.

"Why the rush? Thought the delivery wasn't until tomorrow night." The second guard sounded annoyed.

"Harrison's orders. Someone compromised the network. He's shutting down all external comms after this final transmission. Wiping the servers."

Destiny's eyes widened. She looked at Rubben, understanding the implications. Any evidence of Harrison's operation—including proof of her father's murder—would disappear.

"Go to the salon," Rubben whispered, his decision made. "Keep Harrison distracted. Buy me time."

"You're going to the comms room," she stated. Not a question.

He nodded. "Last chance to get proof. Last chance to call for backup." His eyes locked with hers, intensity radiating from him. "Can you handle Harrison alone?"

The guards' footsteps were moving away now. Destiny straightened her shoulders, the emerald at her ear catching the light.

"I've been handling monsters at poker tables my whole life," she said, a cold determination hardening her features. "Just make it count."

They separated at the next junction. On impulse she ducked into her cabin and thumbed the Iridium again. Nothing. Blank screen, no constellation handshake. The blackout was still total. Good—whatever Rubben was doing, it was a pin-hole, not a doorway. Destiny exited and continued toward the glittering trap of the salon, Rubben slipping silently toward the service stairs that would take him to the belly of the ship. The endgame had just accelerated, and they were now playing on separate tables.

Chapter 7 – Final Table

D estiny took her seat at the final table. The salon, once a temple to excess, now felt like a velvet-draped mausoleum. The vast oval expanse of polished dark wood gleamed under the intense spotlights. Only four chairs remained. Hers. Harrison's at the head. Shark Williams slumped to her left, fingers resting on his meager stack of chips. To Harrison's right sat one of his silent enforcers – the one with the scar bisecting his eyebrow – playing not for chips, Destiny knew, but for blood. Celeste stood behind Harrison's shoulder, her silver dress catching the light, her posture rigid, her tablet clutched like a shield. Her eyes held a distant look, fixed somewhere beyond the table.

Destiny placed her hands flat on the cool felt, forcing her breathing into the slow, measured rhythm her boxing coach had drilled into her years ago. *In. Out. Control.* Her chips, a substantial fortress built on bluffs and reads, felt like meaningless clay tokens. The real stakes were measured in breaths and heartbeats, punctuated by the muffled thump-thump-thump of gunfire echoing through the deck. Distant, contained, but unmistakable. Rubben. Fighting his way through the belly of the beast towards the comms room, towards a distress signal that might never be sent. Every percussive burst vibrated in her bones, a frantic counterpoint to the salon's oppressive silence. *Stay alive. Just stay alive.*

Harrison dealt the first hand himself, his movements fluid, precise, the massive diamond on his pinky finger flashing cold fire under the lights. His dark eyes met Destiny's across the table, a predator acknowledging prey he intended to savor. "The final tableau, Ms. Rivers," he murmured, his voice a low, resonant purr. "No more distractions. Just thee and me now. And the settling of old debts."

The cards slithered across the felt. Destiny picked hers up without looking, her gaze fixed on Harrison's face. Pocket eights. She saw the faint dilation of his pupils. Strong hand. He bet aggressively, a mountain of chips pushed towards the center. The guard called instantly, his expression blank. Shark folded with a shaky hand. Destiny paused, letting the silence stretch, listening to the muffled gunfire below. *Thump. Pause. Two rapid thumps.* Her pulse hammered, a frantic bird against her ribs. She met Harrison's gaze. Saw the predatory gleam. He wanted her to call. He wanted her chips. She tossed her cards face down. "Fold."

Harrison's smile widened a fraction, a silent *I told you so*. He flipped over Ace-King, raking in the pot. "Prudent. But caution can be its own cage, Ms. Rivers." He stacked the chips with meticulous care. "Your father understood that. He was never one for cages." He dealt the next hand, his eyes never leaving hers. "Brilliant man. Saw patterns others missed. Like you." He tapped his temple. "A shame he couldn't see the pattern of his own demise."

The words were a scalpel, probing the raw wound. Destiny's fingers tightened on the edge of the table. She saw Harrison's satisfaction, the cruel enjoyment he took in twisting the knife. She forced her expression into a mask of bored indifference, channeling the cold fury into focus. *He wants you to react. Don't give him the satisfaction.* She looked at her cards. Queen-Jack suited. Harrison bet again. The guard folded. Shark hesitated, his watery eyes darting between Destiny and Harrison, then folded with a sigh. Destiny called, matching Harrison's bet. The flop came Ten, Seven, Four – rainbow. No help. Harrison bet again, larger this time. Destiny calculated the odds, the size of the pot, the distant, sporadic gunfire. *Thump. Silence.* Her breath hitched. *Rubben?* She pushed the thought down. She called. The turn card: a useless Three. Harrison shoved a massive pile of chips forward. "All in." His voice was calm.

Destiny stared at the bet. Calling was mathematically foolish. But folding felt like surrender. She met Harrison's gaze, searching for the tell. The micro-expression of confidence. It was there, buried deep, but present. She glanced at Shark. His stare was fixed on his own folded hands but his right thumb was pressed hard against the table edge. A signal? A nervous tic? Or... a warning? *Bluff.* The thought was sudden, instinctive. Shark knew Harrison's tells better than anyone. He was risking everything, signaling her. *He's bluffing.* Destiny's heart slammed against her ribs. Trusting Shark was insane. But trusting her own read of Harrison's arrogance felt equally perilous. The gunfire had stopped. The silence below was more terrifying than the noise.

She looked back at Harrison, at the cold certainty in his eyes. She pushed her entire stack forward. "Call."

Harrison's expression didn't change. He flipped his cards. King-high. Nothing. A pure, stone-cold bluff. A murmur ran through the few observers. Celeste's intake of breath was audible. Destiny showed her Queen-Jack, claiming the massive pot, doubling her stack. Shark kept his head down, but his shoulders slumped, as if releasing a held breath.

Harrison leaned back in his chair, steepling his fingers. He didn't look angry. He looked intrigued. "Impressive, Ms. Rivers. Very impressive. Marcus would be proud." He dealt the next hand, his movements slower, more deliberate. "He had that same... reckless courage. That belief he could outthink the inevitable." He glanced at Shark. A cold finger traced its way down Destiny's spine. "Of course," Harrison continued, his voice dropping to a conversational murmur, "courage without wisdom is just another form of suicide. As your father discovered." He nodded towards Shark "And as James is about to rediscover."

Before Destiny could process the threat, Harrison's expression hardened. Then he moved. Faster than his size suggested. His hand dipped beneath the table and came up holding a sleek, black pistol fitted with a suppressor. He didn't aim. He didn't shout. He simply pointed it across the table and fired. The sound was a soft, wet *thwip*. Shark jerked violently in his chair. A small, dark hole appeared in the center of his forehead. His eyes widened in surprise, then went blank. He slumped forward, his face hitting the green felt with a soft thud, blood pooling darkly around his head. His whiskey glass toppled, spilling whiskey that mingled with the crimson spreading across the table.

Chaos erupted. Celeste screamed, stumbling back as her tablet clattering to the floor. The guard with the scar stood up, his chair scraping loudly, his hand going to his own weapon. Destiny froze, her breath trapped in her lungs, her eyes locked on Shark's lifeless form. Sacrificed for a signal she'd barely understood.

Harrison ignored the commotion. He kept the suppressed pistol resting casually on the table, pointed in Destiny's general direction. His other hand dealt the next hand. Cards skimmed across the blood-slicked felt near Shark's head. "Your play, Ms. Rivers," he said, his voice calm, untroubled, as if he'd merely swatted a fly. "Let's see if your luck holds. Or if your father's curse finally catches up."

Destiny's hands trembled as she picked up her cards. King-Ace. The best possible starting hand. It felt like a sick joke. Across the table, Harrison studied his own cards, a faint smile playing on his lips. He pushed a stack of chips forward. The guard folded instantly. Destiny forced her numb fingers to push her call forward. The flop came King, Queen, Nine. Harrison made another aggressive be,. Destiny raised, pushing more chips in. Harrison called. The turn: a useless Two. Harrison checked. Destiny placed a large bet, trying to project strength she didn't feel, her eyes fixed on the blood slowly creeping across the felt towards her chips. Harrison called again. The river: another King. Destiny stared at the three Kings on the board. Full house. Harrison checked.

Destiny looked at her hand. Ace-King. She should shove. Push everything. Win the tournament. Win her freedom. But Harrison's pistol rested on the table, a deadly promise. He wasn't playing poker anymore. He was playing executioner. She met his gaze. His dark eyes held a chilling certainty. He knew what she held. He was waiting.

"All—" Destiny began, her voice hoarse.

Harrison moved. Not towards his cards. Towards Celeste. He lunged from his chair, grabbed her arm before she could flee, and yanked her in front of him. He pressed the suppressor of his pistol hard against her temple. Celeste froze, a whimper escaping her lips, her eyes wide with terror, fixed on Destiny.

"Fold," Harrison commanded, his voice flat, absolute. His gaze locked onto Destiny's. "Fold the hand, Ms. Rivers, or watch Ms. Montenegro discover the true meaning of 'all in. Your choice. Your father's legacy... or hers."

The world narrowed to the muzzle pressed against Celeste's skin, to the woman's terrified eyes, to the three Kings on the board mocking her. Destiny's hand hovered over her chips. Fold the winning hand? Or condemn Celeste to death? The cold fury that had sustained her warred with a sickening wave of helplessness. She'd come for vengeance. Not to sacrifice another victim. Her father's face flashed in her mind – not the ghost of her grief, but the man who'd tried to expose Harrison, who'd died trying to stop him. Would he want this? Another death on his conscience?

She opened her mouth, the word "fold" forming on her tongue.

"EMERGENCY PROTOCOLS ACTIVATED! HULL BREACH DETECTED!"

The automated alarm shattered the deadly standoff. Simultaneously, Celeste's tablet—dropped but not broken—began emitting a series of urgent beeps. Its screen flashed with emergency notifications that caught Harrison's attention.

In that moment of distraction, Celeste's eyes met Destiny's. Something passed between them—understanding, desperation, resolve. Without hesitation, Celeste lunged for the emergency station near the windows.

"What are you doing?" Harrison snarled, his composure cracking for the first time.

"What I should have done years ago," Celeste replied, her voice surprisingly steady as she yanked down a hidden lever. "I sent the distress signal when Morrison died. Not just to anyone—to everyone. Coast Guard, DEA, Interpol. With the ship's full manifest and cargo details." Her fingers flew across the emergency panel. "And now I'm making sure you can't escape."

Harrison's face contorted with pure, incandescent fury. "You worthless, treacherous—" He swung the pistol away from Destiny, aiming it at Celeste.

In that split second of distraction, Celeste acted. With a strength born of terror and fury, she twisted violently toward the control panel near the windows.

Harrison ignored her momentary escape, his rage focused on the betrayal. He fired. Thwip! The bullet struck the panel beside Celeste's head, sending sparks flying, but she kept her focus, kept her fingers working the emergency systems. "They're boarding! Now!" she gasped as she slammed her palm against the final protocol button.

Harrison snarled, taking aim again. Destiny moved without thought. She snatched up Shark's fallen whiskey glass and hurled it with all her strength. It struck Harrison's gun hand just as he fired. The shot went wild, punching a hole in the ceiling. The pistol clattered to the floor.

Before Harrison could recover, before the guard could react, the entire yacht lurched violently. It wasn't the gentle roll of the sea. It was a massive, groaning shudder that threw everyone off their feet. Destiny slammed into the edge of the poker table, pain exploding in her ribs. Harrison crashed into his chair. Celeste, who had reached the control panel, was thrown against it, her hand slamming down on a large, red button marked 'EMERGENCY HULL SEAL – SECTOR 7'. Klaxons blared to life, a deafening, pulsing wail that drowned out all other sound. The lights flickered wildly, then died, plunging the salon into near darkness lit only by the emergency strips along the floor, casting long shadows. From deep within the ship came a terrifying sound of rending steel, followed by the chilling rush of water flooding in.

Chapter 8 - Going Under

The grand salon of the *Royal Meridian* was dying. The emergency lights flickered erratically. Klaxons pulsed like a dying heartbeat. The terrifying groan of stressed metal mingled with the chilling rush of water pouring in through the breached hull seal Celeste had triggered. The yacht listed sharply to starboard, sending chairs sliding, glass shattering, and Destiny staggering against the tilting table. Across the carnage, Harrison roared, shoving Celeste aside as she scrambled away. His massive frame, silhouetted against the panoramic windows that now showed only churning black water, radiated pure fury. His eyes locked onto Destiny, burning with the promise of annihilation.

"One hand, Harrison!" Destiny shouted, fighting to be heard over the chaos. She braced herself against the table's edge, the cold water rising past her calves. "Just you and me! All in!" She gestured wildly at the flooding ruin. "You win, you walk. I win..." She met his gaze, channeling every ounce of icy defiance she possessed. "...you stay and drown with the rest of your ghosts!"

It was the ultimate bluff. She had no cards. No chips left worth claiming. Only the desperate gamble that Harrison's monumental ego and his pathological need to win would override his survival instinct. She saw the calculation warring with the rage in his eyes. Saw the flicker of contempt, of disbelief that she dared challenge him now. Saw the predatory gleam that couldn't resist the crushing victory.

His laugh bellowed over the chaos. You think you can beat me now, gyal?' He gestured at the chaos around them. 'Fine then! Your father's arrogance for your life. We deal!'"

He lunged for the scattered cards near Shark's body, his movements clumsy on the tilting deck. Water sloshed around his thighs. Destiny's heart hammered. Every second without Rubben was a gift. She watched Harrison fumble, cursing, snatching up cards slick with blood and seawater. He slammed cards face down before them on the submerged felt, three more between them. In the churning water, random faces and suits appeared - meaningless symbols in their terminal game.

Harrison roared, water spraying from his lips. 'Bet!' He shoved an imaginary pile forward. Your life, dat's what mi betting!'

Destiny didn't look at her cards. She kept her eyes locked on his face, searching for the micro-tell, the flicker of confidence or uncertainty. His pupils were dilated wide with adrenaline and fury. Pure aggression. Pure gamble. Just like his King-high bluff earlier. He thought he held power. He thought the sinking ship was his ally, forcing her hand.

"Call," she said, her voice surprisingly steady in the maelstrom. She met his bet with nothing but her gaze.

He flipped his cards with a snarl. Ace of Spades. King of Clubs. He grinned, a rictus of triumph in the flickering gloom. "Read dem and weep, Rivers! Your father legacy end right ya, tonight!"

Destiny slowly turned over her cards. A deuce and a three. Different suits. The statistical worst hand in poker. Harrison's triumph faltered for a split second, replaced by confusion, then dawning, volcanic rage. She hadn't even looked. She hadn't played the cards. She'd played *him*.

"You... you *bluff* me?" The Jamaican lilt in his voice completely overtook his speech as rage and disbelief merged. 'Bloodclaat! You dare bluff me?' The disbelief in his roar would have been comical in any other circumstance, but was instantly drowned by a more terrifying sound – a monstrous metallic shriek from deep within the yacht, followed by a violent lurch. The floor dropped out from under them. Destiny was thrown forward, crashing into Harrison's legs. He stumbled, off-balance on the sharply angled deck. The emergency lights died completely, plunging the salon into near-total darkness, lit only by the ghostly green glow of the exit strips now underwater.

In the suffocating blackness, punctuated only by the screams of the dying ship, a figure surged through the salon doorway, silhouetted against the marginally lighter corridor beyond. Rubben. He moved like a specter, water churning around his knees, his gaze instantly finding Destiny struggling to rise near Harrison's feet. Harrison recovered faster, his rage honing his reflexes. He lunged not for Destiny, but for the sleek, dark shape of the pistol he'd dropped earlier, half-submerged near Shark's body.

Rubben was faster. He closed the distance in two strides, tackling Harrison low and hard just as Harrison's fingers brushed the weapon. They crashed together into the waist-deep water with a tremendous splash, vanishing beneath the surface. Destiny scrambled back. She couldn't see, only hear the thrashing and the impacts muffled by water. Bubbles erupted on the churning surface.

A hand grabbed her arm. "Come on!" he yelled over the din. Celeste was already there, clinging to a doorframe, her face a mask of terror. Destiny resisted, her eyes fixed on the roiling water where Rubben and Harrison fought.

A head broke the surface – Rubben, gasping, blood streaming from a cut above his eye. Harrison erupted beside him, roaring, a length of broken chair leg clutched like a club in his fist. He swung wildly. Rubben ducked, the wood whistling past his ear, and drove a fist into Harrison's ribs. Harrison staggered back, crashing against a bulkhead already buckling under the immense pressure of the flooding hull. Rivets popped like gunfire. A spiderweb of cracks raced across the metal.

Harrison pushed off, ignoring the groaning wall, his focus solely on Rubben. He charged, the makeshift club raised for a killing blow. Rubben braced, ready to meet him.

But Destiny saw what neither man could—the pattern of fractures spiderwebbing across the bulkhead, the rivets straining against catastrophic pressure. Her poker player's mind calculated odds in an instant. The bulkhead wouldn't hold, but Harrison's momentum could be used against him.

"Rubben, drop!" she screamed, lunging forward.

As Rubben instinctively ducked, Destiny grabbed a broken chair leg floating nearby and swept it hard against the weakest point of the buckling metal—exactly where the stress patterns converged. The impact was minimal, but perfectly timed and placed.

The bulkhead groaned, then shrieked. Harrison, mid-charge, turned his head toward the sound—his momentary distraction giving Rubben time to roll aside. Harrison's eyes locked with Destiny's for one frozen second. She held his gaze without flinching, the same steady calculation in her expression that had cost him millions at the table. His face registered the final, devastating realization—he'd been outplayed.

The panel gave way with an explosive crack, unleashing a torrent of seawater that slammed Harrison backward. The massive metal section, torn free by the force of the inrushing sea, collapsed inward, pinning him against the twisted frame behind it. Water surged over him, around him. His eyes, wide with disbelief rather than fear, remained fixed on Destiny as the dark water closed over his head, churning where he was trapped, only his outstretched hand, fingers clawing futilely at nothing, visible for a second before it too was swallowed by the flood.

Rubben lunged, not towards Harrison, but towards Destiny. He grabbed her arm, his grip iron-strong, hauling her towards the corridor where Celeste waited. "GO! NOW!" he roared over the apocalyptic noise. The water was chest-deep now, rising fast, the current pulling them towards the gaping maw where Harrison had vanished. Destiny stumbled, her feet sliding on the slick floor. Rubben half-dragged, half-carried her through the doorway into the marginally shallower water of the corridor. Celeste grabbed her other arm. Together, they pulled her forward.

The yacht groaned again, a death rattle that vibrated through the deck plates. The tilt increased dramatically. They were running uphill now, towards the stern, fighting the water pouring down the corridor, towards the emergency exit Celeste was frantically pointing to.

"This way! Service ladder to the upper deck!" Celeste shouted, her operational knowledge of the yacht proving crucial. "The evacuation protocols are active—Coast Guard should be here by now!"

Crew members rushed past them in the opposite direction, towards lifeboats Destiny knew were already swamped or inaccessible. Rubben shoved a screaming man aside who tried to grab Destiny. "Keep moving!" he yelled.

They reached a service ladder leading up to a higher deck. Rubben boosted Destiny up first. She scrambled onto the grating, turning to help Celeste, who followed with surprising agility despite her terror. Rubben came last, water cascading off him. The deck they stood on was tilting at a terrifying angle, the stern rising as the bow plunged deeper. The cold night air hit them. The sky was clear, stars brutally indifferent above the chaos. The ocean churned below, littered with debris. The distant wail of sirens cut through the groans of the dying ship – Coast Guard cutters, closing fast but still agonizingly far away.

"We need to get higher! To the helipad!" Rubben shouted, pointing towards the stern superstructure, the highest point still above water. The deck shuddered violently beneath their feet. A lifeboat davit nearby tore free with a shriek of metal, crashing into the churning water below. They ran, slipping on the wet deck, clinging to railings as the yacht's death throes intensified. Reaching the base of the superstructure stairs, Destiny looked back. Harrison's tomb was completely submerged, vanishing beneath the churning water. A final, convulsive shudder ran through the Royal Meridian, and the stern began its slide beneath the waves.

"Jump!" Rubben commanded. "Now! As far out as you can!"

Destiny didn't hesitate. She took a running leap off the tilting deck, plunging into the shockingly cold embrace of the ocean. She kicked hard, fighting the pull of the sinking ship. Celeste splashed down nearby with surprising agility for someone who'd spent years in stilettos and designer dresses. Rubben jumped last, a dark shape against the dying lights of the yacht. The current pulled them together.

"Just keep swimming!" Celeste gasped, her composed façade completely gone, replaced by raw determination. "I activated the emergency transponders—they'll find us!"

Destiny treaded water, her eyes fixed on the spot where the Royal Meridian had been. Only swirling debris remained. Harrison's empire was gone, swallowed by the sea that had been his chosen domain.

Strong hands grabbed her under the arms. Rubben, treading water beside her, holding her up. His face was pale in the starlight, blood still trickling from his forehead, his green eyes wide with adrenaline and a fierce, desperate relief as he scanned her face. "You okay, Destiny? Are you hurt?"

She tried to speak, but only a choked gasp came out. She nodded mutely, her teeth chattering. The cold was seeping into her bones. Celeste was nearby, her survival instincts proving stronger than her refined exterior had suggested. The Coast Guard sirens were louder now. Powerful searchlights swept across the dark water, illuminating the bobbing heads, the wreckage, the oil slick spreading like a bruise.

A rigid-hulled inflatable boat (RHIB) sliced through the waves towards them. Figures in orange survival suits hauled them aboard with strong, efficient hands. Wrapped in coarse emergency blankets, shivering uncontrollably, Destiny huddled on the hard deck of the RHIB as it sped towards the waiting cutter. Rubben sat beside her, his arm a solid, warm presence around her shoulders. Celeste sat opposite them, her perfect makeup gone, her designer dress ruined, but her eyes clear with something like peace—or perhaps the beginning of redemption.

Celeste met Destiny's gaze. "He deserved it," she said. "All of it." It wasn't an apology, not yet. It was a statement of fact, a shared truth between three people who had survived the same monster. Destiny gave a single, slow nod. In that moment, they weren't a poker player, a spy, and a criminal. They were the last players at a table that had just been swept clean.

A woman approached them. She was small with sharp features and dark hair pulled back severely, emphasizing the exhaustion in her eyes. She wore a dark windbreaker over practical clothes, but her bearing screamed authority. Rubben stiffened beside Destiny, his arm dropping away.

"Agent Kane," the woman said, her voice crisp, devoid of warmth. "Mia Young. DEA." She held out a badge, her eyes flicking to Destiny, then to Celeste, then back to Rubben, assessing. "We need to debrief. Immediately." Her gaze lingered on Celeste. "All of you."

Rubben's expression was granite. "Mia." The name was a curse, a question, an accusation.

Young's gaze didn't waver. "It's over, Rubben. Harrison's gone."

"You fed him information." Rubben's voice was ice. "People died because of what you gave him."

Chapter 9 – Triple Agent

Young's jaw tightened. "His network is collapsing as we speak. Assets frozen, associates scrambling."

"You betrayed us." Rubben's fists clenched at his sides. Destiny felt the rage radiating from him.

"Yes, I fed him intel." Young's composure cracked slightly. "Enough to keep him confident. Enough to make him think he owned me."

"Why?" The single word from Rubben carried years of trust destroyed.

Young's eyes flashed. "Harrison didn't just threaten my family, Rubben. He had an asset inside the DEA—someone who fed him my sister's location, my mother's medical records. He owned my entire life before I even knew I was in the game."

Destiny watched the conflict play across Rubben's face—betrayal warring with understanding.

"I played his game better than he did," Young continued, softer now. "Became the perfect double agent..."

"So you could be the perfect triple agent," Destiny finished, seeing the pieces fit together.

Young's attention shifted to her, expression softening. "Your father, Marcus Rivers, was working with us too. He was a good man. A brave man." She reached out as if to touch Destiny's arm but stopped herself. "His sacrifice wasn't in vain. Neither was yours tonight."

The revelation landed like a depth charge. Destiny stared at the small woman, unable to form words as the helicopter's rotors drowned out all thought.

Celeste stepped forward, her composure returning despite her bedraggled appearance. "I have everything," she said quietly, pulling a small, waterproof case from inside her ruined dress. "Every transaction. Every weapons shipment. Every murder." Her eyes found Destiny's. "Including Marcus Rivers."

Young's attention snapped to Celeste, surprise momentarily breaking through her professional mask. "You kept records?"

"I kept insurance," Celeste corrected, a hint of her former confidence returning. "Some of us plan for the future." She glanced at Destiny. "Some of us try to make amends."

Destiny stared at the woman who'd stood beside Harrison for years, who'd watched players eliminated, who'd maintained the perfect facade—and who, in the end, had found the courage to tear it all down. The grief for her father and for all Harrison's victims was still there. But now, there was also the possibility of justice.

The next hours blurred into a haze of shock, cold, and procedural numbness. Medical checks on the cutter. A helicopter flight to a mainland hospital. Endless questions from grim-faced federal agents in sterile rooms that smelled of antiseptic and anxiety. Destiny answered mechanically, her body present, her mind adrift. The images replayed on a loop: the blood on the felt, Shark's vacant eyes, Harrison's hand vanishing beneath the black water, the crushing cold of the ocean. Rubben was kept separate, whisked away into deeper debriefings. Destiny was alone.

She spent three days in the hospital. Not for her physical injuries, which were minor, but for observation—shock, they called it, though the word seemed inadequate for the seismic shift she'd experienced.

In the quiet hours between nurse visits and bland meals, Destiny lay in the white hospital bed, watching shadows move across the ceiling. Sleep came in violent bursts—nightmares of black water rushing in, of Harrison's hand reaching for her through the flood, of her father's face morphing into Rubben's, then into Harrison's. She would wake gasping, sheets twisted around her legs like the yacht's wreckage.

During daylight, memories surfaced like debris—Shark's vacant eyes, Alex's blood on white tile, Celeste's terrified face in the searchlight's glare. The clean, antiseptic smell of the hospital couldn't wash away the lingering scent of seawater and oil that seemed embedded in her skin. Nurses offered sedatives. She refused. The poker player in her needed clarity, needed to process each hand exactly as it had been played.

On the second night, she finally wept. Not the controlled tears she'd permitted herself at her grandmother's funeral, but gut-wrenching sobs that came from somewhere primal and long-sealed. She wept for the twelve-year-old girl who'd been told her father died in an accident. For the years spent constructing armor made of mathematics and probability. For the father who hadn't abandoned her but had been stolen from her.

"He died protecting people," she whispered to the empty room, testing the weight of this new truth. "He died fighting." The words felt foreign on her tongue, a language she was only beginning to understand.

By the third day, something had settled in her. The grief was still there, but it was clean now. Purged of the poison of doubt and abandonment. In its place was something unexpected—a fierce pride. Her father had made choices that cost him everything. Had sacrificed himself rather than become what Harrison embodied. The emerald earrings she'd worn for seventeen years weren't just jewelry; they were a legacy of courage she'd carried without knowing.

As the sun set on the third day, she stood at the window, watching the lights of the city below. She was Marcus Rivers' daughter. Not just in blood or name, but in the choices that defined her. In the unflinching calculation of risks. In the courage to call a monster's bluff even as the waters rose.

On the fourth day, a lawyer visited. An elderly man with kind eyes and arthritic hands that carefully arranged a folder of documents on the hospital tray table.

"I'm Walter Gaines," he said, adjusting his wire-rimmed glasses. "I worked with your father for nearly twenty years."

Destiny's heart skipped. "You knew my dad?"

He nodded, a sad smile crinkling his weathered face. "Marcus was... well, he was something else. Brilliant man. Cautious, except when it came to you."

He tapped the folder. "Your father left something for you, Destiny. Not money—though God knows he could've used more of that—and not property either. Something trickier." He leaned forward. "There's a safety deposit box in Zurich. Can't be accessed without your fingerprints and this."

He pulled out an old-fashioned key, holding it between them.

"What's in it?" Destiny asked.

"His journals. Digital drives—encrypted, of course. Documentation of his work with the DEA." Walter's voice softened. "The truth, kid. That's what he wanted you to have when you were ready."

He hesitated, turning the key over in his fingers. "Look, I should warn you... this stuff, it's not just history. It could be dangerous. Marcus documented networks that Harrison only fronted for. People who'd... well, who'd rather stay in the shadows."

"So I'm still a target," Destiny said flatly.

"Maybe. Or..." Walter smiled slightly. "Your dad always said you had his mind. His guts too. This information could be a foundation for something else. A way to finish what he started. If that's what you want."

He placed the key in her palm, closing her fingers over it. "Your choice, Destiny. Always was."

Weeks turned into months. Destiny returned to Las Vegas, to her minimalist apartment overlooking the glittering, indifferent Strip. The $10 million prize was gone, swallowed by the sea and Harrison's collapsed empire. She sold the apartment. The view felt hollow now. She used the money to buy a smaller place that was quieter and less exposed. She started training again – not just boxing, but firearms and surveillance detection. The lawyer's words echoed. *Dangerous. A target.* She visited her father's grave for the first time since she was a child. She placed the emerald studs beside his headstone. "I understand now, Dad," she whispered to the quiet earth. "I see what you saw." She left them there, a final offering, a symbol of wisdom passed on. She wore simple studs now.

Six months later, she walked into the Aria. Not to play. Just to feel the hum of the place, the electric thrum of risk and calculation. Old habits died hard. She moved through the crowds, anonymous in dark jeans and a leather jacket, her senses alert, cataloging tells and bluffs at the tables she passed. She was scanning the high-stakes room, more out of professional curiosity than intent, when she saw him.

Rubben Kane.

He stood near a roulette table, not playing, just observing. He looked different. Leaner, harder. The shadows under his eyes were deeper, but the intensity in his green gaze was the same. He wore a dark suit, impeccable but somehow less like armor than before. He turned, as if sensing her stare. Their eyes met across the crowded floor. Time seemed to stutter, then snap back into focus. The noise of the casino faded to a distant murmur. The pull was immediate, like the visceral recognition of a perfect hand after hours at the table. It wasn't just attraction; it was recognition. Of shared terror. Shared survival. Shared lies that had become a twisted kind of truth.

He started walking towards her. She moved to meet him. They stopped a few feet apart, the space between them charged with everything unsaid, everything survived.

"Destiny." His voice was deeper. "Fancy meeting you here."

"Rubben." Her own voice was steady, despite the sudden acceleration of her pulse. "Just taking in the atmosphere. Seeing if the house edge still holds."

He nodded, his eyes searching hers. "It always does. Eventually." He paused, the casual words hanging in the air, heavy with subtext. "Can I buy you a drink? Somewhere... quieter?"

The connection was still there, forged in the crucible of the *Royal Meridian*. But so was the memory of betrayal, of secrets kept, of the dangerous legacy she now carried. They weren't the same people who had boarded that yacht. The innocence was gone, replaced by a hard-won, scarred understanding. Trust wasn't a given; it was a choice they'd have to make anew, moment by moment. And the world outside wasn't safe. Harrison's network was shattered, but the darkness he'd thrived in still existed. His associates. His rivals. People who might want revenge. Or the secrets Marcus Rivers had died for, now resting in a Zurich vault.

"Just one drink," Destiny said, matching his small smile with one of her own. It felt tentative. "See where the cards fall."

He offered his arm, an old-fashioned gesture that felt strangely right amidst the casino's neon glow. As she slipped her hand into the crook of his elbow, her fingers brushed the hard outline of a compact pistol holstered beneath his jacket. Her own jacket shifted slightly, the weight of the small Glock snug against the small of her back a familiar, necessary comfort. They walked towards the quieter bar, two survivors navigating a world that would always hold shadows, their steps in sync, their guard never fully down. The game had changed. The stakes were different. But they were still playing.

Thank you VERY much for reading my book. If you like this story please read more of my books at books2read.com/garveyavon